"I don't want to be any man's mistress."

Philippa stared at him, her face pale and her eyes dark. "Least of all, yours."

"Do you know something, Philippa?" Mark looked down at her reflectively. "You'd be much better off as my mistress than anyone else's. At least I understand you. One day, that repressed sensuality is going to break out, my dear, and make your life hell if the wrong man, or at least one who doesn't understand you, gets in its way."

"If anything," she whispered, "could be less calculated to make me change my mind, you've just said it."

He pushed his hands into his pockets with a shrug. "So be it." His voice was mocking. "We'll keep the battle lines drawn...."

LINDSAY ARMSTRONG married an accountant from New Zealand and settled down—if you can call it that—in Australia. A coast-to-coast camping trip later, they moved to a six-hundred-acre mixed-grain property, which they eventually abandoned to the mice and leeches and blackflies. Then, after a winning career at the track with an untried trotter, purchased "mainly because he had blue eyes," they opted for a more conventional family life with their five children in Brisbane, where Lindsay now writes.

Books by Lindsay Armstrong

HARLEQUIN PRESENTS

1071—RELUCTANT WIFE
1095—WHEN YOU LEAVE ME
1183—HEAT OF THE MOMENT
1295—ONE MORE NIGHT
1327—A LOVE AFFAIR
1439—THE DIRECTOR'S WIFE

HARLEQUIN ROMANCE

2582—PERHAPS LOVE
2653—DON'T CALL IT LOVE
2785—SOME SAY LOVE
2876—THE HEART OF THE MATTER
2893—WHEN THE NIGHT GROWS COLD
3013—THE MARRYING GAME

LINDSAY ARMSTRONG

Leave Love Alone

Harlequin Books

TORONTO • NEW YORK • LONDON
AMSTERDAM • PARIS • SYDNEY • HAMBURG
STOCKHOLM • ATHENS • TOKYO • MILAN
MADRID • WARSAW • BUDAPEST • AUCKLAND

Harlequin Presents first edition September 1992
ISBN 0-373-11487-7

Original hardcover edition published in 1991
by Mills & Boon Limited

LEAVE LOVE ALONE

Printed in U.S.A.

CHAPTER ONE

'NAKATCHAFUSHI,' Philippa Wright read when she should have been doing something else, 'is ninety leisurely minutes by *dhoni* from Hulule Airport. . .Yes?' She looked up at the girl standing beside her desk.

Jennifer Smith was a pretty blonde, about five feet two, and Philippa was instructing her on the new computer system she'd installed in the Brisbane offices of the Learmonth Group—had been instructing her until Jennifer had decided they could do with a cup of coffee and gone away to get them. Which was when Philippa had pulled the travel brochure from her capacious pocket and started to read about the Maldive Islands.

'He's arrived,' Jennifer said out of the corner of her mouth and put two paper cups down on the desk with hands that shook visibly. In fact her whole small person was buzzing with barely concealed excitement. 'And he's heading this way.'

Philippa slipped the brochure back into her pocket. 'Who has arrived and is heading this way?' she asked idly, and settled her large, horn-rimmed spectacles more firmly on her nose.

Jennifer looked at her exasperatedly. 'Mark Learmonth! Who else? I told you this morning that he's making a tour of all the companies in the group because, so they say, he could be taking over from his father as——'

'Who else, indeed,' Philippa murmured drily and added, 'Shouldn't we then at least give the impression that we're working, Jenny?'

Jennifer sat down beside her hastily and said with a giggle, 'I just hope he doesn't ask for a demonstration—I go all goose-flesh when he's around. So will you probably—I don't believe there's a girl alive who doesn't. He's just gorgeous,' she said dreamily.

'Want to bet?' Philippa replied tartly.

'You wait!' Jennifer threatened.

In the event they didn't have long to wait.

A sudden hush came over the office as the door opened and all eyes but Philippa's swivelled towards it, all hands but hers were arrested, and Jennifer sighed audibly. Philippa went on punching keys stoically—she was not after all an employee of the Learmonth Group, and there was more than one reason why she didn't have to join the Mark Learmonth Admiration Society—but she was also not quite as stoical as her appearance indicated.

In fact as she stared at the screen before her, she was thinking, I wonder if he has any idea that I've become heartily sick of the mere mention of his name and I couldn't have cared less that Mark Learmonth was a genius at just about everything he turned his hand to, not to mention his prowess with *women*? Nor could I care less that he's turned all his genius to taking over the Learmonth Group from his father. Who cares?

Consequently, when the entourage stopped at her desk—a fact that was indicated to her by Jenny's involuntary wriggle of excitement—she punched a few more keys before looking up coolly.

And straight into a pair of equally cool grey eyes.

'Er—this is Miss Wright, Mr Learmonth,' the head of the department, Max Walker, said just a shade anxiously. 'Of Colefax and Carpenter, the company that won the contract to instal the new computer program. Miss Wright is at present instructing Miss Smith——' he indicated Jenny, who beamed widely '—who has been with this department for—two years, Jenny?'

Jenny tripped to her feet and said breathlessly, 'Oh, yes! Well, *nearly*, and I do love every *minute* of it.'

Philippa winced inwardly for Jenny and waited for Mark Learmonth's reaction, at the same time conscious of a tinge of surprise because Mark Learmonth was not quite what she'd expected. But then what had she expected? A cross between Tom Cruise and Rudolf Valentino? No, that was ridiculous—what, then? Something flashier, a more overpowering physical presence? Yet the man beside her undoubtedly *had* a presence, and he was tall although not bulky, and definitely good-looking but in a different way from what she'd expected, and yes, she could briefly understand why Jenny was breathless and inarticulate—but couldn't she *see* the indifference in those grey eyes?

He said nothing, however, but smiled faintly at the other girl then turned his attention back to Philippa.

'How do you do, Miss Wright?' he murmured. 'Len Colefax is a friend of the family, although I haven't seen him for a while. How is he?'

'So far as I know, he's fine,' Philippa replied. 'We don't see a lot of him ourselves.'

One dark eyebrow lifted at her. 'Do I detect a note of disapproval, Miss Wright?' Mark Learmonth queried, and Max Walker moved restlessly.

'No, merely a statement of fact, Mr Learmonth,' Philippa said evenly. 'It's not my place to approve or disapprove——'

'Er—Miss Wright,' Max Walker intervened hastily, 'would you care to demonstrate the particular system you're working on at present?'

'Well, I should imagine it would be a pointless exercise unless Mr Learmonth has a basic *grasp* of the program, but if you like,' Philippa said with a shrug.

An audible gasp ran round the room and Jenny whispered her name imploringly. But Philippa continued to hold that cool grey gaze with her own until she had the satisfaction of seeing a slightly dangerous glint replace the indifferent coolness. Then she stood up, patted her black, mannish jacket—which topped a plain white blouse, a long grey skirt, black tights and flat black shoes—into place, and offered Mark Learmonth her chair.

That was when he got his revenge. He was still taller than she was, which surprised her dimly again, and he took his time—as if he had all the time in the world to look her over, to take in her tightly scraped-back hair, the large plain glasses, her thick, garish make-up, her clothes which gave the impression of a bulky figure and were badly cut, and finally her flat black shoes and battered document case beside the desk.

Then he looked up again and that same faint smile twisted his well-cut lips as he said, 'Do you carry a cane in your briefcase by any chance, Miss Wright?'

'You did *ask* for it,' Jenny was still saying dazedly half an hour later.

Philippa shrugged with pretended indifference although *she* was still raging inwardly. 'I can't stand men who think they're God's gift to women,' she said shortly. 'And he's not my boss so I don't have to kowtow to him, and the only thing that should concern him is how good I am at my job—which is pretty good,' she added wearily. 'Look, can we just forget all about it? I know to you I must seem like a creature from another planet, but there's a good reason for it. And the less men like Mark Learmonth *like* me, the better it is for my career.'

'But he's here for another three weeks,' Jenny

said helplessly. 'So are you. If it were me, I'd curl up and die every time I laid eyes on him.'

Philippa turned her head and regarded the other girl with a sudden smile. 'That's where we're different, Jen, but don't worry about it. I can cope!'

Yet that evening, at home in her pleasant flat in an old and leafy suburb of Brisbane, Philippa found those words haunting her.

Her flat was the upstairs floor of an old house that had been renovated, and it was spacious with high ceilings and polished wood floors. The walls were ivory and held her budding art collection in lovely splashes of colour or serene pastels, there were Persian rugs on the floor and some exquisite antique pieces of furniture and ornaments that she'd collected at home and abroad.

It was in her jade and white bedroom that she put her battered briefcase down when she got home and immediately started her nightly after-work ritual—and realised that she was still upset by the encounter with Mark Learmonth.

The first step of the ritual was always the exchanging of her spectacles for contact lenses, the scrupulous cleaning of her face then a change of clothes—tonight into a crisp buttercup blouse tucked into white shorts. Then she released her hair. Once down from its restraining combs and clips, it sagged dispiritedly to her shoulders, but as she brushed it steadily it revived, and began to ripple and glint in a cloud of living chestnut.

She put her brush down and stared at herself in

the mirror, marvelling, although rather cynically and not for the first time, at the transformation and how she'd become so adept at creating two Philippa Wrights. This one, who, with her greenish eyes, oval face, soft, smooth skin, long legs, narrow waist and beautifully curved hips and breasts could grace any calender, she'd been told, not much to her pleasure—and the other Philippa Wright, terror of offices with her brisk, aggressive manner, mannish clothes, awful make-up.

'It does the trick every time,' she murmured to herself. 'And *no one* can deny now that I've achieved what I have without the help of any man. No one can say Philippa Wright has used her pin-up girl qualities to get where she has——' she glanced around at her paintings and antiques, thought of her bank balance and the holidays she took each year '—and no one can insinuate that she has only one purpose in life—to be leered at and fondled and taken to bed. So why,' she asked herself thoughtfully, 'should the fact that Mark Learmonth swallowed the bait—hook, line *and* sinker—upset you? Because he retaliated where many only laugh behind their hands? Because he's not. . .quite what you expected?'

She stared at her reflection unseeingly as she examined this thought with a faint frown. She had certainly formed the impression that Mark Learmonth would be the kind of man she liked least: over-confident, too well aware of his effect on others and particularly some women—yet he'd been the opposite, indifferent until called to arms and with a quality that was hard to define. . . Unless that was it, she mused, quality and very adult. But who was to say that underneath those quiet good looks he was not just like most men? And why the hell she was bothering herself about it, she couldn't imagine!

She kept this thought well entrenched in her mind as she made herself dinner then spread some work out on the dining-room table.

The phone rang, and she glanced at her watch and sighed because it would be her mother, she knew. She rang twice a week on the same nights at exactly the same time.

'Philippa,' her mother said after a few minutes, 'I want you to come to dinner this week—*please*, darling, this feud with your father has gone on long enough and you won't even tell what it's about this time!'

'Mum—you should know by now without having to be told, we've "feuded" ever since I can remember,' Philippa said ironically and, she hoped, evasively.

'I know your father is not an easy man to please, pet, and I know it always hurt you that he should recognise Ray's achievements and be. . .well, a bit offhand about your own, but. . .'

A *bit*, Philippa raged inwardly as her mother rambled gently on. Don't you know it's on *your* behalf as much as my own that I. . .detest him sometimes? What would you say if I told you that this latest feud was sparked off because I saw him with my own eyes, wining and dining a woman, caressing her with his eyes in an unmistakable prelude to the real thing—and she's only one in a long line of many? Don't you know or care? How can you not—why do we have to play these games?

'Mum,' she said wearily. 'Oh, all right.'

But the fact that her mother finally rang off, sounding pleased, didn't stop her from brooding about her tall, distinguished father who had aged so much better than her gentle, faithful, *devoted* mother; her father who, despite his preoccupation with and use of women for sex, basically despised their brains and was fond of accusing dedicated career women of getting to the top on their backs. His contempt—or was it a mixture of contempt and guilt? she sometimes wondered, since he was a successful businessman himself and, paradoxically, was certainly in the position to advance a few careers—was never more clearly demonstrated than when he'd recommended his only daughter to get married and start a family rather than pursue a career, although she'd consistently got better grades at school and university than her older and only brother Ray. Another womaniser, she thought bitterly. Perhaps he not only took lessons from Dad but also from Mark Learmonth when they were at university together, and he was so impressed with the guy and the way the girls adored him?

She closed her eyes and grimaced, and wondered if her father would ever lose the power to hurt her, then she decided she was being introspective and gloomy and that was generally a sign that she needed a break, and she retrieved the Maldive brochure from her jacket with a sudden sense of anticipation. For, while Philippa Wright might be clever and a lot of things some considered unwomanly, she was also an incurable traveller, and the more romantic, far away and unspoiled the place, the better she liked it.

She made the booking for her holiday and paid the deposit the next day during her lunch hour, made an appointment to have the first of two typhoid shots and to start a course of anti-malaria tablets, and thought, I've just got to get through the next six weeks until the twenty-seventh of November. That shouldn't be too hard; in fact the *last* three weeks should be a breeze. . .

Two days later she was summoned to Mark Learmonth's office.

Max Walker brought the summons himself and accompanied her to the top floor of the building, which housed the executive offices.

It was obvious to Philippa that Max was slightly ill at ease as they rode up in the lift, and she said suddenly with a rather wry smile, 'It's all right, Max. I don't intend to let this encounter get out of hand. What does he want to see me about?'

'He didn't say precisely.'

'He must have given you some indication.'

Max shrugged. 'Well,' he paused and shot her a glance, 'he *has* said he's very pleased with the program you've put in and I think he'd just like to discuss it with you. Philippa——'

She broke in serenely, 'Don't worry, Max. I'd have been very surprised if he hadn't come up with some way to show me he does have a basic grasp of these things.'

Max Walker rolled his eyes. 'That's what I was afraid of. Philippa——'

'But if you think I'm going to go on playing this game of tit for tat, I'm not, Max,' she interrupted again and added, 'We're here, Max.'

'God help us,' Max Walker muttered but, when she laughed, he grinned faintly too and said, 'I doubt if even he can beat you on your own ground—provided you just stick to it,' he added entreatingly.

Mark Learmonth was sitting behind a beautiful mahogany desk across a sea of royal blue carpet as they were ushered into his office. He glanced up immediately, then reached for the phone that buzzed beside him and waved them to pull up chairs.

He spoke only two words into the phone. 'Yes, right,' and put it down saying to Max at the same time, 'That was your office, Max. You're needed back there urgently.'

'Oh! Well. . .' Max glanced at Philippa and hesitated, his indecision plain for all to see.

'It's all right, Max,' Mark Learmonth said placidly, leaning back in his chair. 'I doubt that Miss Wright and I will come to blows, but I can always call on my secretary for assistance if the need should arise.'

Max Walker sighed audibly, lifting his shoulders, and he left—but not without another warning and entreating glance at Philippa.

But Philippa was staring at her hands in her lap and calling on every ounce of will-power she possessed to stop herself from doing just that—well, from rising swiftly and slapping Mark Learmonth's good-looking, indifferent face. But, at the same time, she was still reeling mentally from the wholly unexpected impact coming into his presence had had on her. The ridiculous awareness that had assailed her as soon as she'd stepped into the room and seen him sitting easily behind the desk and invested but lightly with the power of the position—or perhaps investing the position with his indefinable air of quality; the *curious* awareness of the way his grey jacket highlighted the fact that his shoulders were broad, although not unduly so, that his white shirt and discreetly patterned tie appealed to her taste, that his hair was brown and thick and glossy and his hands were beautiful, long and probably strong. . .

The silence lengthened and a full minute passed before she was able to raise her gaze and feel assured that she only looked expectant as she said, 'I believe you wish to discuss the program?'

His grey eyes studied hers. 'Actually, I wanted to congratulate you, Miss Wright. I believe you wrote it yourself.'

'Not entirely. The problem-analysing and the

input-output format designations were a team effort at Colefax, but the algorithm was mine and I did the testing and debugging.'

'And handled the transfer from the previous system and trained everyone here to handle it,' he said. 'By the way, Len Colefax is in town and he is well,' he added. 'He also speaks very highly of your—ability, Miss Wright.'

Philippa raised her eyebrows briefly, for several reasons. Len Colefax, despite *his* ability, was an older version of exactly what she'd pictured Mark Learmonth to be, and she knew very well that she would never have been taken seriously at Colefax and Carpenter without her disguise. She also knew that Len Colefax disliked the kind of woman he thought she was, but could not fault her work. So he tolerated her on a personal level and gave her, on a business level, the most complex problems he could find, no doubt secretly hoping she would fall flat on her face one day. But she hadn't, and her reputation was growing slowly but steadily.

She said without thinking, and from subconscious motives it took a long time to define, 'I should imagine what he really said was, "If you can stand the battleaxe, she's not bad at her job"—or something along those lines.' She stared defiantly into Mark Learmonth's cool grey eyes.

For a moment they didn't change, then he smiled, with genuine amusement, and Philippa caught her breath and could have shot herself.

If he noticed, he gave no indication, but picked

up a pen and swung it between his fingers, saying wryly, 'You two know each other well, by the sound of it.'

'We. . .tolerate each other,' Philippa said carefully.

'Wouldn't it be better working for someone you liked?' he queried.

Philippa smiled. 'No.'

He gazed at her thoughtfully then took her by surprise. 'How old are you, Miss Wright? Twenty-four?'

'How——?' She stopped abruptly.

'Did I guess? I'm not sure,' he said slowly, as that idle grey gaze wandered at will over her. 'Something to do with your wrists and your ankles,' he said meditatively then. 'They don't quite seem to fit the rest of you. Nor do you have to cover them up,' he added gravely as she moved and instinctively pulled down her sleeves. 'I have no designs on them.'

His soft words fell into a little pool of stunned silence then Philippa coloured and, of course, bridled. 'It wouldn't do you any good if you did,' she said tartly. 'Besides, I don't see how you can tell a person's age that way, so——' She broke off and bit her lip.

'So you immediately assumed I had an interest in them? What a very uncomfortable life you must live, Miss Wright,' he said ironically, 'if you spend most of it imagining things like that.'

Philippa gasped, choked and started to declaim hotly, but it all came out in an awful tangle. 'I *don't—if* I do it's not without cause, believe me, *Mr* Learmonth, and I've no doubt you're no different from most men in your own quiet way——' She stopped again but this time because he was laughing quietly. But worse was to come.

He stood up and came round the desk to half sit on it, facing her with his arms crossed and his eyes still ironically amused as he said, 'Oh, I am, Miss Wright. Definitely no different from most men. I believe women are to be enjoyed in a certain way, which I probably don't have to describe to you, but then again, who knows? Have you never allowed a man to——' he paused and studied her thoughtfully '—take out all that armoury you wear in your hair and run his fingers through it? Never felt a man's hand on your breasts or——?'

'*Stop* it!' she commanded hoarsely and incredulously.

He lifted an eyebrow. 'I wonder if that means yes, you have or no, you haven't—if it's the latter, why don't you give it a try one day? It might reverse a lot of your opinions of us,' he said gravely.

Philippa swept to her feet. 'Before you say another *word* on the subject, Mr Learmonth,' she said icily, 'may I remind you that I could cause utter chaos downstairs if I so chose, because if I can iron the kinks *out* of the system, believe me, I can also do the reverse——'

'I'm sure you could, Miss Wright,' he said on another note altogether, a dangerously even note that was curiously more effective than any emphasis, 'but I doubt if your reputation would survive the furore that would follow.'

'*Oh*. . .' Philippa ground her teeth more from sheer exasperation that she should have allowed herself to be goaded into uttering a threat that was totally alien to her ethics. . .

'Do I see the light of reason striking you, Miss Wright?' he followed up ruthlessly. 'If so, Len Colefax need not hear of your threat, but otherwise. . .' He shrugged.

Philippa clenched her fists then deliberately relaxed them. 'I'll tell you what you see, Mr Learmonth,' she said contemptuously. 'You see someone who heartily despises you but at the same time is *damned* if this won't turn out to be the best program the Learmonth Group has ever had. As for the cheap, crude sexual overtones you managed to introduce into the conversation, you're lucky——'

His teeth glinted in a lightning smile as he interrupted, 'Did you think I was recommending myself? Do forgive me, I was merely giving some general advice. As for your program——'

'But the success of it still hinges on one other thing, Mr Learmonth,' Philippa spat at him, as enraged as she could not recall ever having been before. 'That I don't have to lay eyes on *you* again.'

She swept out.

CHAPTER TWO

BUT the next morning Philippa was back in Mark Learmonth's office, his outer office at least, and if she was rather pale no one could tell.

She had also browbeaten his attractive secretary into accepting that Mr Learmonth would see her without an appointment, although the girl had insisted she must wait until his phone call to Sydney was over. 'It's his father,' she'd said rather desperately. 'No one interrupts old Mr Learmonth.'

'Very well, I'll wait,' Philippa had replied and sat herself down on the comfortable, elegant couch.

She was dressed much the same as she always was at work—she had a whole wardrobe of baggy, shapeless clothes to call on now—but today, instead of black or grey and white, she wore a peculiarly unpleasant khaki. Which, she reflected as she smoothed her skirt, suited her peculiarly unpleasant state of mind. And she sighed as she recalled snatches of the sleepless night she'd spent, and snatches of her mental turmoil.

It was supremely ironic, she'd thought at one stage, lying wide-eyed in the dark and even finding it grimly amusing, that he should—no, that *I* should have played the part so perfectly. The stereotyped version of a neurotic spinster, convinced that most men have deep, dark, awful designs on them. But the really ironic part is not that I allowed myself to be trapped into playing the part so well, but that I reacted so incredibly then. Oh, God, perhaps that's what I'm becoming? A neurotic spinster. . .

She came back to the present with a grimace and once again reminded herself that *that* particular turmoil had nothing to do with her professional ethics, and it was only because of those that she was here now.

Right on cue, a red light glowed on the secretary's small console, she spoke into it briefly then said to Philippa, with some surprise, 'Mr Learmonth will see you now, Miss Wright.'

'This is a surprise, Miss Wright,' Mark Learmonth said coolly, leaning back in his chair. 'Do sit down.'

'Thank you. But I'd rather stand,' Philippa replied crisply, and laid a long white envelope on his desk. 'This is my resignation, and I'm tendering it because I feel I've compromised my professional ethics. I delivered a similar letter to Colefax this morning, explaining that it was no longer possible for me to continue with this assignment.'

'That's certainly a change of heart,' Mark Learmonth said drily after a moment's silence.

Philippa shrugged.

'*Are* you doing this for professional and not—personal reasons, Miss Wright?' he said then, and his grey eyes held a glint of mockery as they locked with hers.

'Purely professional reasons, Mr Learmonth,' she answered quietly. 'I made a threat yesterday, in the light of which I don't see how you can ever have complete confidence in my program again, and I've laid myself open to your suspicions if the program *should* ever break down. It's just not feasible to continue in those circumstances.'

He sat up. 'You also gave me to understand yesterday that I *could* have complete confidence in this program—but we'll deal with that separately. How will this effect your position with Colefax, Miss Wright?'

Philippa shrugged again. 'That will be for Mr Colefax to decide. This shouldn't, however, cause you too much inconvenience. There will still be the expertise at Colefax to take over from me.'

They stared at each other, Philippa taut in every line of her figure, he alert, dispassionate—and dangerous, damn him, Philippa thought suddenly, and she took a deep breath to calm herself.

'I——'

'I really don't feel,' he overrode her, 'that towering over me will serve any purpose in this conversation, Miss Wright. Please sit down.'

It was said smoothly and quietly but with a cutting edge that briefly got the better of Philippa. She hesitated but sat, and one part of her mind wondered how he did it—again without emphasis—while another taunted her for being a coward. So she said, from her chair, 'I don't believe there's much more to converse about.'

'Then I'm afraid I differ.' He picked up his phone and instructed his secretary to get Len Colefax on the line.

Philippa tightened her lips, which he observed with a faint twist of his own as he began speaking into the phone.

'Len? Yes, it's Mark Learmonth again. . . Fine, thanks. Len, I believe you got a letter from your Miss Wright this morning, indicating that she could no longer continue with this program she's installed for us. . . Yes, well, something of a surprise to us too, but I'd like to let you know that we don't believe she's compromised her professional ethics at all and that from what I've seen of the program, and her training programme, I really wouldn't be happy about swapping horses mid-stream, so to speak. . . No. . . No, we're all most impressed, I can assure you. Would you like to speak to her yourself?' He held out the phone to Philippa.

Pure incredulity had lit Philippa's greenish eyes as the one-sided conversation progressed, and her lips were still parted as she stared at the phone in Mark Learmonth's hand. Then her nostrils flared as she stood up and took it from him. 'Hello?'

'Philippa,' Len Colefax growled down the line, 'what the hell is going on?'

'I——' Philippa licked her lips '—thought I was doing the right thing,' she said and stopped.

'It seems to me you haven't been thinking much

at all,' Len barked. 'Don't you realise what your program could lead to? That it's a pilot series and if it's successful—well, hell, Learmonth's is a big group and who could say what would follow? Don't tell me,' he said in suddenly weary tones. 'Someone's been making a pass at you—I always knew women were nothing but trouble, but I thought you were the *one* who wouldn't have that trouble—what the hell is going on?'

It was Philippa's turn to swear, but beneath her breath, and to find herself with sudden tears of mortification in her eyes, which caused her to say curtly and with sharp defiance, 'All right. I'll finish the job.' And to abruptly hand the phone back to Mark Learmonth.

She didn't really hear the rest of the conversation as she prowled towards the window and stood with her back to the desk, so great was her angry confusion, but it didn't last long. She did hear the silence finally and forced herself to turn round.

She also said, 'Well, you win. I'd better get back to work.'

Their gazes clashed across the room, then Mark Learmonth said unhurriedly but with his same indefinable purpose, 'Sit down again, Miss Wright. I may have won the war but the peace has yet to be delineated. It might help,' he added musingly, 'if we were to wonder together how this storm in a teacup blew up into such a war.'

Once again Philippa hesitated but couldn't escape the mesmerising power of those cool grey eyes, and once again she sat down reluctantly, this time thinking dully that he might have a point.

She clenched her hands, then tried to relax. 'I insulted you, you insulted me and hit upon a spot where I'm probably over-sensitive,' she said drily, 'and bingo! That's how it all started, Mr Learmonth.' She gazed at him challengingly.

'That's fairly fair,' he said thoughtfully. 'But I can't help wondering why you were moved to insult me barely moments after you'd laid eyes on me for the first time ever—to my knowledge.'

Philippa said with a weary little gesture, 'Look, if this is going to be an exercise in making me squirm, I already am—I allowed my prejudices to speak for me rather unwisely, that's all. Speaking figuratively, I'll pick someone my own size next time. Can I go now?'

'Your prejudices against men?' he queried idly.

'*Yes*. As if you didn't know,' she added. 'As for your advice, going out and getting myself "laid"—I think that's the crude term for it—never solved anything in my estimation.'

'That is a very crude term for it,' he agreed mildly. 'Much cruder than any I used and not specifically what I had in mind. *Allowing* yourself to love someone and be loved—something along those lines was what I was suggesting.' His grey eyes held hers gravely.

Philippa couldn't prevent the colour that began to steal up from the base of her throat, so she stood up without permission and said brusquely but with a nerve beating visibly in her jawline. 'You amaze me, Mr Learmonth, you really do. Do you take this kind of interest and initiative with all your female employees? I'm only surprised the Sexual Discrimination Board hasn't heard of you yet. Still, we live and learn, and I'm going back to work whether you like it or not.'

He stood up himself and walked around the desk and to the door, which he opened for her politely and with a completely sober expression except for a faintly wicked glint in his eyes. And he waited until she was abreast of him to say softly, 'Only those in need, Miss Wright.'

Philippa stopped mid-stride, glared up at him and was about to tell him furiously that he'd gone too far when, with her lips parted and her eyes flashing, she was overcome by the knowledge that she was making a fool of herself—and that he was enjoying seeing how much further she would rise to the bait. . . *Damn*. She looked away and felt herself colouring and bit her lip with annoyance.

'You were going to say, Miss Wright?' He lifted an eyebrow.

'Nothing. I. . .' But she could only lift her shoulders helplessly, and reluctantly lift her eyes to his.

That was when it happened again, the one thing she'd congratulated herself on, the small mercy in this débâcle—that no curious awareness of Mark Learmonth had overtaken her.

But now it did, in spite of the insults he'd traded with her, in spite of his manipulation of her, in spite of everything, she thought with a stunning little sense of shock. And it caught her and held her standing with only inches between them, a physical impact that came not only from his tall proximity but the sheer knowing that he was dangerously attractive and she *was* like every other girl and not immune to those austere good looks. Not immune to his well-cut mouth or to glancing involuntarily down to his long, strong, beautiful hands and wondering what it would be like to have them on your body, touching your breasts, those cool grey eyes intent on what he was doing to you, those discreetly broad shoulders beneath your lips. . .

To her horror, she broke out into a sudden sweat that beaded her temples, and she felt her pulses come throbbingly alive—and she moved convulsively to go through the doorway.

But he said, 'One last thing, Miss Wright.'

Philippa stopped and could only say huskily, 'What?'

'I do admire your professionalism.'

She stared at him, searching for mockery in his gaze, but there was only what they'd started out with: polite indifference.

She murmured, 'Thank you.' And escaped.

She found it very difficult to concentrate for the rest of the day, then remembered with a further sense of exasperation that she was having dinner with her parents. True to form it was a severe test of her goodwill, and made even harder when her mother enquired about her latest assignment, which she always did as if to compensate for

Philippa's father's lack of interest. But it seemed he was interested this time.

'Learmonth's, eh?' he said genially, leaning back with his wine. 'You'll need your wits about you, Pip. I believe Mark Learmonth is a much tougher businessman than his father, and that's saying something! I remember Ray was most impressed with him when they were at university together, although Ray was a bit younger——'

'And quite a bore on the subject,' Philippa said tartly before she could help herself.

Her father sat up and said less genially, 'You'd do well to pay heed, nevertheless, Philippa, and also recall that you were only a scrubby schoolgirl at the time. In fact it mightn't be a bad idea to let him know you're Ray's sister, it could only help.'

'Darling, I——' Philippa's mother tried to intervene but she was brushed aside.

'Don't get *too* cocky, Philippa,' her father warned. 'Remember that old saying about pride——'

'Coming before a fall,' Philippa finished for him sardonically and was about to add that she wouldn't when she was suddenly sharply reminded of the mauling her pride had taken at Mark Learmonth's hands in the last two days. Well, she thought bitterly, point taken, and how I could have imagined an attraction to a man who is not only a friend of my *brother's* but needs to be treated with all the caution one would accord a—snake, is beyond me. And she returned to the attack obliquely.

'How is Ray?' she enquired smoothly.

There was a small silence, then her mother said sadly, 'He's in Fiji on a holiday. He's broken up with Jessica.'

'And about time too,' her father said moodily.

'But they've been living together for two years!' her mother objected.

'That doesn't mean she was the right one for him—oh, the girl was pretty enough, but too temperamental if you ask me.'

Poor Jess, Philippa thought. It was probably two years of hell, and what have you got to show for it? Being damned with faint praise, but if only you'd known what to look for, the signs were all there. . .Ray uses women and always has, some of my schoolfriends among them—it's a case of like father, like son, talking of old sayings—and for a moment she wanted to fling that one at her father. But she veiled her gaze and said instead, 'I think it's a good thing too. Better now than after they were married.'

'She's probably heartbroken, though,' Mrs Wright said softly.

The fact that her husband and her daughter retorted in the same breath that Jessica would get over it, then glared at each other, increased her agitation, which Philippa noticed as she was about to open her mouth to say something along the lines that some women deserved all they got. She closed her mouth and took a deep breath, and put her hand over her mother's. 'She probably will also get over it, you know. Have I told you about my holiday?'

And she made a determined effort for the rest of the evening, even during her father's homily on how well Ray was doing in his career as a civil engineer, before taking herself home exhausted.

But she woke up the next morning feeling grimly amused at the mere thought of using her brother's name to ingratiate herself with Mark Learmonth. She was not to know that the thought was to become fact.

Two days later, Max Walker again brought her a summons to the top floor.

'What is it this time?' she said irately.

'It's a managerial meeting and——'

'That's got nothing to do with me,' she broke in impatiently.

'All the same, he wants you to give a progress report on your work—there are several policy decisions coming up it could affect.'

'With so little notice? What does he think I am—a machine?' she queried acidly.

Max Walker forbore to comment but he murmured that she did have half an hour to make some notes.

'And so,' Philippa said to the eight men seated around the table in the boardroom. 'I can confidently predict that all the remaining problems are now minor ones and the program will be off and running within the time-frame we estimated.' She named a date about two weeks off.

Mark Learmonth rose. 'Thank you, Miss

Wright, that was very succinct and impressive and I think this would be a good time to break for lunch. We'll reconvene at two, gentlemen.'

Philippa started to pack her notes away as a general exodus occurred but Mark Learmonth said quietly, 'Could you spare me a few more minutes of your time, Miss Wright?'

Her hands stilled, then she shrugged.

He waited until the room was empty and strolled over to a window to stare down at the street for a time before he turned and said with a faint smile, 'I believe I know your brother.'

'How. . .?' Philippa stared at him.

'I seem to recall now that someone mentioned Ray had a brainy sister.'

'So—and because of the name—is that how you linked us?' she said disjointedly.

'No. I've just remembered that—in fact your father rang me——'

'He *didn't,*' Philippa whispered. 'He *wouldn't.*'

Mark Learmonth lifted an eyebrow. 'I can assure you he did. What's the problem? The old school tie bit is an established custom and I don't see why it shouldn't be extended to sisters.'

'If you think,' Philippa said in a raging undertone, 'I have any desire to be included in your old school tie bit or that this is anything but an attempt on my father's part to *patronise* me on his own and my brother's,' she said with contempt, 'behalf, not to mention *yours,* you're quite mistaken.'

All the amusement drained from Mark Learmonth's expression. 'I had no patronage in mind,' he said coolly.

'Didn't you?' she shot back at him. 'Try this—are you sure it didn't occur to you to think, well, she seems to be an odd kind of sister for Ray Wright but I might take a kinder view of her eccentricities instead of making such fun of them? Well, I'll tell you now, Mr Learmonth, there is no need. Just go on being the way you were—at least it's your true colours!'

'I'll tell you what *has* just occurred to me—it's Philippa, isn't it?' he said and continued as she drew a breath, 'Are you jealous of your brother Ray, Philippa?'

'You're damn right I am,' she retorted. 'I would also scorn to be the kind of woman who runs after him—and you,' she said scathingly, 'from what I've heard!'

'Are you quite sure you're not also dying to go to bed with me, Philippa?' he said softly but with such cutting irony, she flinched.

'How dare you?' she breathed.

'I dare because I can't help wondering what's really causing all this—emotion. So——'

'Excuse me,' a voice said tentatively behind them.

They both swung round to see a fair girl standing in the doorway.

'Susan,' Mark Learmonth said wryly. 'How long have you been there?'

'I've just come. Your secretary said she was sure you were finished, but if I'm interrupting anything——?' She smiled at him and her whole face lit up with a look of radiance.

Philippa stared at her and saw that she had an enchanting, heart-shaped face, deep blue eyes, a lovely figure, and discovered she herself couldn't help feeling overgrown and graceless by comparison. She also couldn't help thinking bitterly, She's obviously dazzled by him but she's so young! I hope she doesn't think he's the one for her. . .

'No, you're not,' Mark Learmonth said. 'Miss Wright and I can continue this later.' He turned to Philippa. 'Can't we, Miss Wright?'

Philippa gritted her teeth. 'Once again, I think we might have said it all, Mr Learmonth,' she murmured, 'so——'

'On the contrary, I think there are a few more points to cover before we put the subject to—er—bed. I'll be in touch.' He turned back to the other girl. 'Well, Susie, what brings you to town today?'

Thus dismissed, Philippa left because the alternative was to stay and make an awful fool of herself by completely losing her temper.

The next days were not only very busy, as she strained every nerve to ensure her program's success, but filled with tension in case he should make good his threat and 'be in touch'. Not that she had any intention of allowing him a final encounter, and as the days progressed even began to think it had been an idle threat and she needn't be constantly on guard. But when she was tired out and unable to censor her thoughts, she couldn't help wondering how whatever it was between them had blown up to such proportions, and she knew she was afraid of Mark Learmonth now, and his uncannily acute perceptions.

And when he did achieve a final encounter in a typically treacherous male manner, she knew she'd been right to be afraid.

He entered the large office she was working in and the inevitable hush greeted his arrival, so every word he said to her was clearly audible to everyone around. He said with an enigmatic smile, 'Miss Wright, I believe you only have a few days left with us?'

'Yes,' Philippa answered uncertainly.

'Then as a token of our respect for your efforts over the past weeks, I'd like to invite you to have lunch with me in the directors' dining-room.'

An audible gasp rippled round the office, then everyone held their breath and every eye was riveted on Philippa.

For the life of her, all she could manage to say foolishly was, 'Now?'

He glanced at his watch. 'It's just about your lunchtime, I believe. Do you have a prior appointment? If so we could make it tomorrow.' He waited.

Philippa licked her lips. 'No. I. . .that is. . .' She trailed off lamely.

'Good,' he said gravely. 'Allow me to lead the way.'

CHAPTER THREE

THE directors' dining-room was not large, but it was subduedly luxurious with the glint of crystal and silver, and it was empty.

'If you'd care to freshen up, there's a powder-room through there,' Mark Learmonth said. 'Can I order you an aperitif?'

Philippa opened her mouth, closed it, then said, 'Yes, I will freshen up, and yes, thank you, I would like a dry sherry.'

But in the powder-room she wondered why she'd bothered going there, although she washed her hands, because there was not a lot more she could do and it filled her with a cold sense of despair to find that she hated her reflection in the mirror. Then she squared her shoulders resolutely and returned to the fray.

A white-coated steward described the lunch offerings and took their orders and melted away so that once again the room was empty but for them.

She picked up her sherry and sipped it. 'If this,' she said slowly, 'is going to be more of the same, may I make a simple statement and a request?'

'You may,' he said, and leant back in his chair with his gaze resting inscrutably on her face.

She fiddled with her glass for a moment. 'The

way I am, which appears to activate a—shall we say—twisted sense of chivalry within you, to put it as kindly as I can, really need be no concern of yours. *I'm* not particularly concerned, you see, although I am suitably chastened for the insult I first offered you. I'll certainly think twice before I again allow my prejudices to speak for themselves, and—here's the request bit—could we just leave it at that?' She looked up at last and for a moment to her surprise thought she detected a glint of admiration in his eyes.

But when he spoke, she knew she must have imagined it. He said amusedly, 'You're not going to admit anything, are you, Philippa? Not even to yourself, but never mind, I'm getting a bit weary of it all too. What should we discuss? The weather? Our last holidays or the next; as a matter of fact mine is coming—what's the matter?' he said in a different voice as she put an involuntary hand to her mouth.

'Nothing,' she said indistinctly and took a deep breath.

'You looked—for a moment you looked quite distressed,' he said with a frown in his eyes.

'Perhaps,' she said with an effort, 'I was wondering why I have to be treated with *such* contempt. There is one thing we could talk about without making a complete mockery of me. For example, you could tell me whether your "respect for my efforts over the last weeks", quote unquote, could mean there's a possibility of my pilot program being extended to other sections of the Learmonth Group. Oh, please don't imagine I'm asking for any firm commitment or that I have any devious or subtle plans to hold you to ransom in any way, but. . .it would be more interesting than the weather.' She drank the last of her sherry, mentally castigating herself for the hurt his words had inflicted and hoping to God his perceptions weren't working as well as they normally did.

The arrival of their meal saved her from his direct comment, but his eyes did linger on her narrowly as the steward placed their plates, and still lingered as a bottle of wine was presented for inspection, until the steward coughed discreetly.

'Yes, that will be fine,' Mark Learmonth said unhurriedly, at last turning that penetrating grey gaze to the bottle. 'Well, Philippa, there is a possibility of that,' he said as the golden Riesling flowed into their glasses. 'I don't know whether you're aware of it but my father is hoping to retire, and the general idea is that I should take up the reins. I,' he paused, 'expect to expand the company and do some streamlining.' He stopped and stared at his wine and she was suddenly struck by the rather sombre set of his mouth.

'You don't—I mean, you seem a little reserved about it all,' she said.

He lifted an eyebrow and his lips twisted. 'I'm not—rather, I've made the decision, but sometimes the thought of all the responsibility involved is—sobering.'

'Is there something you'd prefer to do?' she asked with a sligh catch in her voice.

He grimaced. 'It's too late for that—no, not really. It's what I always expected to do and worked towards. No,' he said with a sudden grin, 'and please don't spread any rumours that I'm thinking of taking to an alternative lifestyle, will you, Philippa?'

She made no effort to conceal the ironic reproach in her eyes. 'Thanks.'

'Sorry. You,' he said meditatively, 'have obviously never reached the stage in your career that comes to most of us, I'm sure, where you—stop and wonder?'

She shrugged. 'No. Well, after our recent run-ins, I did pause, yes, but I decided I needed a break, that's all.'

He laughed. 'I came to the same conclusion—I mean that I need a break in order to infuse some enthusiasm into myself. Here,' he raised his glass, 'let's toast our respective rest and recreational plans in the hope they'll be fruitful, but,' he said with a wicked little glint in his eye, 'before you take offence, perhaps we should steer clear of holidays and the weather. So, you may take it, Philippa, that if all goes to plan and we decide to streamline all our computer procedures, your program will be given top consideration.'

A little inward sigh, like the death of a seed of hope that had never really blossomed, echoed through her, but she raised her glass and managed to smile. 'To R and R. May I pass the news on to Mr Colefax?'

'Yes. I was going to do it myself but if you'd rather.'

'It would give me great pleasure,' she said with relish, and for the next minutes concentrated on her grilled fish.

'There is something I would like to ask you, Philippa,' he said when they'd both finished and she'd declined dessert. 'Why do you hold your father and brother in—quite some contempt, I gather?'

She pleated her napkin thoughtfully. 'One doesn't generally discuss those kind of things with strangers, does one?' she murmured finally.

'One doesn't,' he agreed. 'When one has already let those secrets out in the heat of the moment, however. . .' He looked at her wryly.

Philippa flushed but she said steadily, 'You then regret breaking ranks.'

'And leave people to form their own conclusions,' he countered.

'Mr Learmonth——'

'Don't worry so,' he said softly. 'I always knew your brother was,' he shrugged, 'spoilt, and bore all the trademarks of being the apple of his father's eye. The rest is not hard to guess at all. How long have you been striving to outdo Ray, Philippa? A long time, I would think,' he said before she could speak. 'But I put it to you that the only person you're damaging in this contest is yourself.'

'Mr Learmonth, no,' Philippa said determinedly, and she rose. 'Thank you for lunch, but I must request you to drop this topic otherwise I shall leave. In fact I must leave anyway——'

'Because the truth hurts?' He pushed back his chair and stood up as well.

'Because my lunch hour is over,' she said and fumbled for her bag.

He leant down and got it. 'Then I won't detain you. And I'll kill all my chivalrous instincts of the twisted kind stone-dead in any possible future encounters, Miss Wright. Does that—please you better?' he queried seriously, but there was no mistaking the satirical glint in his eyes.

'Please do,' she said huskily. 'Otherwise there'll be no question of our working together again, Mr Learmonth.'

He smiled unexpectedly. 'Spoken like a truly angry woman. I have to admire your sheer spirit,' he said. 'But don't worry, I think it would be wise if we used intermediaries in any future working relationships. May your career prosper—Miss Wright.' He handed her her bag.

'And yours, Mr Learmonth,' Philippa said huskily. 'May I make one last remark? I can't help feeling you might benefit from being married, you know. It might give you the sense of purpose you lack and protect you from your baser chivalrous instincts.'

For just a moment, she thought that she'd hit home for the first time. His eyes certainly narrowed to a hard, piercing grey as he said, 'As a matter of fact I——' But he paused, then said softly, 'When was marriage ever a safeguard against anything, Philippa?'

And that hit her home base in a way he couldn't begin to guess. She turned away abruptly and left.

In her last remaining days she only saw him once, not to speak to but unable to doubt that what had passed between them was now a closed book, as his gaze drifted over her unhurriedly and as indifferent as it had ever been.

She left Learmonth's and went back to Colefax and Carpenter, where she spent the last weeks before her holiday handing over to someone who would be able to stand in for her should anything go wrong with the Learmonth system. She also resolutely tried to banish Mark Learmonth from her mind and was not unsuccessful at times, but one query kept returning—had he been going to say that he *was* thinking of getting married 'as a matter of fact'? To whom? she wondered. The girl he'd called Susie who'd been unable to hide the fact that just the sight of him made the sun shine? Yet, she couldn't help thinking, he had sounded. . .how? Not particularly lover-like, but that could have been embarrassment. Unless you knew Mark Learmonth, she always reminded herself.

The subject arose again on her last day when she went in to make a final report to Len Colefax, who'd been away since her return to the fold.

'Well, Philippa,' Len leant back in his chair and

studied her curiously, 'as they say, all's well that ends well, but I'd give my eye-teeth to know what happened at Learmonth's. Mark wouldn't elaborate, for reasons best known to himself.'

Philippa smiled mechanically. 'I had a. . .run-in with him, that's all, Mr Colefax. I thought I was renowned for that kind of thing.'

Len Colefax shrugged. 'That must have been a change for him—most women lie down in the aisles for him, and that makes even less sense. I'd have thought you both would have been happy to part company, then.' He eyed her then his gaze sharpened. 'Sure you didn't fall in love with him a little, Philippa?'

Because she'd had over five weeks to debate this with herself, Philippa was well prepared. 'No,' she said coolly and added, 'You know me better than that, Mr Colefax.'

He pursed his lips. 'Well, I thought so, but in case you don't know it, it would be waste of time to fall in love with Mark Learmonth.' He brooded for a moment, then changed tack with some evident relief. 'This holiday you're taking—will we be able to contact you?'

'No,' Philippa said with relish.

'Where the hell are you going?'

'To the middle of the Indian Ocean. . .' She relented a little at his incredulous look. 'To the Maldives. They're a group of twelve hundred or so islands west of Sri Lanka.'

'My dear Philippa, why——?'

'They're supposed to be very beautiful—they're

coral atolls—very peaceful, and a diver's paradise, that's why. And I think I do need a really peaceful holiday.'

'Are you a diver?' he asked, his eyebrows still raised.

'No.' Philippa paused. 'But I love out-of-the-way places.' She smiled at Len Colefax. 'Don't look so anxious. I haven't flipped and I fully intend to come back, so you can look round for something really *testing* for me. In fact, although he made no commitment, Mr Learmonth gave me to understand he's intending to expand and streamline——'

'So he's going to do it!' Len said keenly.

'I've just told you——'

'But do you know what that means, Philippa? He's going to take over Bannister's—yes, go on,' he commanded.

'He didn't say that——' Her eyes widened. 'You mean the merchant bank, *that* Bannister's? Well,' she said as her boss nodded impatiently, 'he said. . .' And she repeated Mark Learmonth's words.

'Philippa!' Len Colefax stood up. 'Is this any time to be going on holiday?'

But she stood up as well and her lips twisted into a wry smile as she held out her hand. 'Most definitely, it is. Happy Christmas in the meantime, Mr Colefax—I won't see you before then.'

That night, after she'd gone through her ritual, she stared at the khaki outfit she'd hung up with the rest of her work clothes, grateful that for the next weeks she wouldn't even have to see them. Then a curious little shiver ran down her spine and she identified it as the forerunner of a decision she had the feeling she was going to have to make: whether to continue with this double life.

'And to decide whether,' she murmured, 'the disguise didn't become the reality. As for Mark Learmonth, well, I've had all that out often enough, and never again will I be superior about the power of a purely physical attraction. But that's *all* it was and it's never enough. So what I have to concentrate on now is my holiday, and how it's going to help me come to terms with. . . myself.'

She spent several days before she left with her parents, and, because it mattered to her mother, was peaceable with her father. She also tried to lay to rest her mother's fears on the subject of the recent coup attempt that had taken place in the Maldives.

'It's all over, Mum, they wouldn't be letting people in if it weren't, and it never spread beyond the capital, Male, anyway. And the Indian Army and Navy have come in to keep the peace.'

'How far away will you be from Male?' her mother asked anxiously.

'Ninety leisurely minutes by *dhoni*,' Philippa replied with a rueful little smile.

'That's another thing—these *dhonis*, are they safe?'

'Yes, they've probably been sailing them—the

same design anyway—in that part of the world since time immemorial and they do look romantic, don't they?' Philippa said patiently as she fished out her dog-eared brochure and showed her mother a picture of a *dhoni*, which was rather like a large graceful gondola but with Arabic lines.

Her mother looked unconvinced.

But after a five-day stop-over in Singapore and four hours of winging her way over the Sumatra Hills and the Indian Ocean, Philippa stepped into the Nakatchafushi Island resort *dhoni* with the Maldivian name of *Thunbibi* painted in white on its blue sides, and was charmed.

A day later she was even more charmed by the Indian Ocean paradise of the Maldives and the small, oval, beach-trimmed and palm-tree-topped island of Nakatcha, as it was affectionately known to all.

She'd never seen beaches so white, sea so clear within the encircling coral reef, where you needed only to wade in to your waist to be surrounded by a myriad tropical fish of every colour of the rainbow. She loved her rondavel—all the accommodation on Nakatcha was in separate rondavels with thatched roofs, white walls, pretty floral curtains and bedspreads, functional bathrooms, and all only steps through lovely shady foliage to the beach.

She'd even made friends with an English couple at whose table she'd been placed, who'd included her in the group of friends they'd made so the awkwardness of being a lone female was not a problem.

In fact, on her second night she was feeling relaxed and happy, and not to know it was all about to be torn to shreds.

The first incident did not actually tear it to shreds, but it happened that very night as she was making her way down the sandy path to her rondavel. The fifty or so people on Nakatcha were a cosmopolitan mostly European crowd, and a lot of them were very serious about their diving. One group of the most ardent divers were four young men, two English, one German and one Belgian, and it was them Philippa chanced to overhear as she passed them sitting on the beach. They were discussing her, quite unaware that, although she hadn't stopped, everything they said was audible as she stepped on to her veranda and then couldn't help herself.

'I tell you she's on her own! She's Australian and——'

'She is a boomer!' This with a German accent.

'Boomer—I think you mean a stunner, Karl. She is that, probably not a good swimmer or a diver but——'

'We know she doesn't dive,' an irritated English voice said, 'but why shouldn't she be a good swimmer?'

'It is, I sink, a question of aerodynamics. A body like that, wis sose marvellous bustens. . .'

'Lends itself to other occupations,' the irritated

Englishman said. 'Her name, incidentally, is Philippa——'

'And sose long legs—did you see her wis the green bikini today? Walking along the beach? I saw sree windsurfers close in fall off seir boards.'

There were several chuckles. Then the second Englishman said gloomily, 'She's probably as cold as a maggot. . .'

Philippa let herself into her rondavel at this stage with a sigh, and then she shrugged philosophically and vowed that she wouldn't let it spoil her holiday.

What did, however, occurred the next day at lunchtime. She'd swum and snorkelled through the house reef, an expedition which had made her very hungry so she'd strolled over to the coffee-shop rather early for lunch.

It was deserted but for a lone male sitting at a table in the corner, whom she ignored as she ordered her lunch from Ali, the friendly Maldivian head waiter. Then, as she waited, she pulled her spectacles out of her beach-bag to read the two-week-old English paper she'd picked up. She always carried her spectacles in case of any disaster with her contact lenses, although today she was only resting her eyes from them.

But it was as she put them on that a familiar voice said, 'Good God! It's Miss Wright.'

CHAPTER FOUR

IT WAS Mark Learmonth, staring at Philippa with his eyebrows raised quizzically and his grey eyes faintly incredulous. Mark Learmonth in shorts and a T-shirt and his brown hair damp—there was no doubt about it, although Philippa blinked a couple of times.

Then she said in a oddly strangled voice, 'What are *you* doing here?'

He grinned faintly and stood up. 'The same as you, probably. May I join you?' And, without waiting for a reply, he pulled out a chair and sat down. 'This,' his still incredulous gaze took in her colourful sarong, which was all she wore over her swimming-costume, her bare, smooth, faintly golden shoulders, her naked face and cloud of shining chestnut hair, 'this is. . .quite a revelation, Miss Wright, if you don't mind my saying so.'

'I can imagine,' Philippa replied tartly, causing him to look amused.

'I take it your stunning metamorphosis doesn't extend to your state of mind,' he drawled. 'Really, I'm almost lost for words. Which is the real you, may one enquire?'

Philippa pulled her glasses off, thereby slightly blurring the outline of his face, and said thoughtfully, 'Do you know, I'm not all that sure any longer, Mr Learmonth, but right now the last thing I want to be reminded of is. . .' She paused.

'The other you?' he took the opportunity to put in softly.

'Yes,' she said flatly. 'I don't suppose it would be any good asking you to go away? There *are* many other resort islands in the Maldives——'

'Ah, but Nakatcha is one of the best, besides which I come here every year—no, no good at all, Miss Wright,' he said gravely. 'We will just have to learn to live with each other. Are you here on your own?'

'Of course,' Philippa replied with a trace of bitterness. 'I don't suppose the same applies to you?'

'Miaow,' Mark Learmonth said barely audibly, causing her to flush faintly, which he studied with unconcealed interest, then he went on, 'I am and I'm not. I didn't bring a sleeping-partner—I can do without it from time to time, despite the fact that you've obviously formed the opposite opinion of me, Miss Wright. But I'm here with my sister and her husband and my nephew. We're all dedicated divers, actually,' he said apologetically.

'I'm amazed,' Philippa said with some truth. 'Incidentally, my opinion had to do with what I was told about you, but now I'll be able to go back and set the record straight, won't I?'

'Ah.' He sat back. 'With your brother Ray, do you mean? Perhaps you should make your own judgements in future.' His grey eyes glinted with mockery.

Philippa took a deep breath and opened her mouth, but he forestalled her. 'I was right about your wrists and ankles, wasn't I? They didn't fit with the rest of you—as was. Want to tell me why you go to such extreme lengths to disguise yourself?'

Philippa stared at him, but the mockery had gone and there was only curiosity in his eyes now. 'I. . .if you had any idea how difficult it is to advance in the business world as a woman, you wouldn't need to ask,' she said at last.

He narrowed his eyes. 'I think that's a bit old hat now, surely.'

'Oh, I think in Australia, anyway, it's alive and well. And not only Australia,' she reflected. 'Just last night I happened to overhear some men discussing how well my person lends itself to one particular occupation.'

He grinned with pure amusement and murmured, 'Men will be men, I'm afraid. And they could be right—it seems to me it would be an awful waste, otherwise. But not all men would expect you to restrict yourself to that one occupation.'

Philippa was saved by the arrival of her lunch—not only hers but Mark Learmonth's as well, which Ali obligingly and with a large beam brought to her table.

But although she was able to restrain herself from throwing her papaya juice over him, she still said precisely, 'I can see we're going to have to devise a formula, Mr Learmonth——'

'Do call me Mark, Philippa,' he said politely.

'Devise a formula,' she said through her teeth, 'so we can both stay on this island without coming to blows, *Mark*. I think it's best if we avoid each other entirely, don't you?'

He raised an eyebrow. 'On Nakatcha? That should be almost impossible. I have a better idea, Philippa.' He paused and said her name again, then, 'It suits you, it's not a *frivolous* name—no, I have a better idea. I think we should get out our white flags. After all, I presume you came here to get away from formulas and programs and algorithms—you told me you needed a break and I told you the same.'

Philippa discovered suddenly that she couldn't see her lunch at all, and not only because she wasn't wearing her glasses but mainly because ridiculous tears were blurring her vision—I *never* cry, she thought fiercely, *why*——?

'Philippa?'

She closed her eyes, reached rather blindly into her beach-bag for a handkerchief, blew her nose and put her glasses on determinedly, then looked up.

To find that his expression had sobered completely. 'Were you crying?' he said abruptly.

'No.'

'Your rather lovely green eyes certainly seemed to have tears in them.'

'They're. . .sore,' Philippa said raggedly. 'That's why I'm wearing glasses and not my contact lenses.'

'I see. I thought for a moment our little sparring

matches had really upset you, but perhaps you actually enjoyed them and that's why you don't want to wave the white flag.'

Her lips parted and she said, '*Enjoy*. . . I think one of us must be going mad. *I'm* staring the ruination of my holiday in the face. *You* might enjoy. . .' She stopped.

'Why?' he said with that alert, dangerous glint in his eye she knew and feared. 'It's not the first time I've tried to wave the white flag—why do you really have such an incredibly low opinion of me, Philippa? So that you automatically assume I've ruined your holiday?'

Trapped. . . The thought ran through Philippa's mind. And, if only you knew. . .

'I'm sorry,' she said huskily and shrugged helplessly, but knew she had to get off this dangerous ground. 'It usually takes me a little while to switch personalities. I've only been here two and a half days. I don't have a white flag on me, I'm afraid,' she smiled and hoped it didn't look as shaky as it felt, 'but perhaps you're right. Peace,' she said solemnly and held up her palm.

For a moment, as he studied her impassively, she thought he wasn't going to accept it, but then the planes and angles of his face relaxed and he said, 'So be it. But, just in case, let's choose a nice safe topic. Are you a diver—Philippa? And your lunch is getting cold.'

'Oh. No. But I snorkel. And I swim rather well despite not having the right aerodynamics. That,' she added hastily as he frowned faintly, 'well, don't ask me to explain, I'd rather not. By the way, when did you arrive? This morning?'

'Yes,' he said after a moment. 'Actually we arrived last night at midnight but it was too rough to come and get us so they put us up on Villingili—not the best introduction to the Maldives.'

'I've heard all about Villingili,' Philippa said with a grin. 'We did have a bit of a blow last night.'

They ate in silence for a while until Philippa said, 'Where is the rest of your family?'

He looked past her. 'As a matter of fact, just about to descend on us.'

Philippa pushed her plate away and her chair back rather awkwardly. 'Well——'

'You don't have to dash off,' he murmured. 'I'm sure they'd like to meet you.'

'I. . .'

But it was too late. Three happy people breezed into the coffee-shop and she found herself being introduced to Mark's sister Julia, her husband Rory and their seventeen-year-old son Gary.

'What a coincidence!' Julia, who was not much like her brother but fair, petite and perhaps a few years older than Mark Learmonth, said gaily. 'A friend from Brisbane so far away—it is a small world.'

Philippa glanced at Mark obliquely. For reasons best known to himself, he had not alluded at all to the fact that they were only business acquaintances—perhaps adversaries would have been even more accurate. And, she thought, friends. . .could it ever be possible?

But despite his sister Julia's gaiety Philippa thought she detected a slight reserve in her eyes although there was none in her husband, a mild, genial man, and young Gary Waterford could think of nothing but his first dive, later in the afternoon. Then she wondered if she'd imagined it as the conversation became general and they exchanged reminiscences about the flight to Male, the thoroughness of the Custom officials, the tall, impressive Indian soldiers everywhere and how much she was enjoying Nakatcha.

But when Rory Waterford invited her to have dinner with them, Julia seconded the invitation a fraction belatedly and Philippa grimaced inwardly and put, as she was to discover, quite the wrong interpretation on it—that it was Rory Julia was worried about falling prey to her charms. Yet it made it easier to decline gracefully and claim a prior engagement. She also stood up, saying ruefully, 'If you'll excuse me, I'm going to be very decadent and have a lovely long siesta. Enjoy your dive—and take care,' she added.

But Mark Learmonth rose too. 'I'll walk you back to your rondavel, then. I don't know about decadent—I think siestas are rather civilised.'

'You didn't have to do this,' Philippa said.

They were strolling along the beach in the direction of her rondavel.

' Nine, ten,' Mark Learmonth murmured. 'I

knew you were going to say that and I guessed it would only be about ten paces before you did.'

Philippa bit her lip. 'I apologise for being so transparent,' she said tartly, however.

He laughed quietly and glanced down at her. 'Who are you having dinner with, by the way?'

It occurred to her to tell him to mind his own business, but two things stopped her. She had, after all, agreed to a truce but, more than that, she had a strange feeling that he simply wasn't going to allow her to get away with anything less—without getting hurt in the process. She said, 'An English couple I've made friends with. They're old enough not to worry about two being company and three a crowd, nor for her to worry about her husband making eyes at me—all the same they're very nice,' she added a little guiltily.

'The pitfalls of being a single girl,' he murmured. 'This seems to be an odd sort of holiday for a single girl to choose,' he added thoughtfully, and stopped her with a hand on her elbow.

Philippa turned to face him with something like a sigh and a wry expression in her green eyes. 'I thought it was agreed I'm a *very* odd sort of girl.'

'Certainly. . .different,' he agreed drily and studied her silently.

It was a hot clear day with the sun almost directly overhead and striking gold off his brown hair, and what *was* odd, Philippa found herself thinking, was that this Mark Learmonth was suddenly more intimidating than the city version of him, then found herself understanding, in the next breath, why.

She moved abruptly. 'What's so different about liking to travel and see the world?'

'Nothing.' He shrugged. 'It's just that on one's own it can be a lonely occupation.'

'I've never found it so,' she retorted. 'Why do men always imagine women either have to be in gaggles or with someone of the opposite sex? *Men* can be loners, can't they? Why not women?'

He smiled suddenly. 'Do you know I can't come up with one plausible reason—not one that would satisfy you, my prickly Philippa——'

'I'm not *your* anything!'

'All right, all right,' he said peaceably. 'I should know by now what a sore spot that is,' he added wryly and, before she could retaliate, took her breath away by observing. 'In view of *this* Miss Wright, it's hard to believe there's never been a man in your life, though. Hasn't there?' he queried, allowing his gaze to travel down to her bare feet and back again, leisurely.

'It has nothing to do with. . .' Philippa took a deep breath, unclenched her jaw and said sweetly, 'I can see your peace of mind is seriously at stake. Yes, there was once but it didn't last very long, I didn't find it particularly satisfactory and nor did he, so we parted, agreeing to disagree on just about everything and quite bemused, I think, about what had attracted us to each other in the first place—— '

'And you let that turn you off men for all time,

Philippa?' he said with amused incredulity. 'Don't you know that a lot of first times, upon reflection, bemuse a lot of people?'

Philippa sighed. 'I have to be honest—*you* bemuse me a lot, Mr Learmonth. All right, let's just go back to square one. I'm. . .a crazed loner and, worse, happy to be so. May I go now?' She turned away but he caught her wrist.

'Like hell you are,' he said softly, 'but yes, you may go. Until next time, that is.' He lifted her wrist and spanned it in his long fingers, then restored it to her side. 'Enjoy your siesta,' he said barely audibly, and smiled briefly down at her.

She didn't enjoy her siesta at all, despite the cool of the air-conditioning and the interesting book she was reading. And she wondered bleakly whether she'd ever enjoy anything again, but that seemed excessively maudlin and, with a flicker of real apprehension, she realised she was feeling lonely—damn Mark Learmonth! And afraid. Because it was one thing to feel a physical attraction at a distance, so to speak, and even that had been powerful enough. But close to. . . And that was why he was even more intimidating, in a way. . . This is ridiculous, she told herself abruptly. It doesn't stop him from needling you, in that certain way that men use when they either want to take you to bed or teach you a lesson. And, she added with sudden decision, when you so much *despise* being at the mercy of your senses, surely you can apply a little mind over matter? A lot, then, but you do have a brain, Philippa Wright, so use it.

Her brainpower, thus called upon, told her to seek refuge in company and activity, and for the next couple of days she did just that. She went on the organised night *dhoni* fishing-trip, and caught a monster of a fish which no one could tell her the name of because the *dhoni* crew were all Maldivian and spoke no English. But it was a jolly trip and, coming back by the light of the stars and watching the light-framed, dark-skinned crew navigating so competently by the stars, she experienced a feeling that was hard to describe. A feeling of timelessness and history—the history of these lovely islands did stretch back to Roman times at least.

The next day she went on the shopping and sightseeing trip to Male, and again was charmed. By the busy, colourful waterfront dominated from the harbour by the golden dome and minaret of the mosque, by the dusty, unmade roads, some lined with white walls and tantalising blue doors, by the thirteen-thousand bicycles and the little schoolgirls, sparkling and neat in white dresses and walking two by two. Even the bullet holes in the white and gold façade of the mosque and the Indian soldiers on the streets were a cause for fascination rather than fear.

And she returned to Nakatcha, happily laden down with silk sarongs, a marvellous woven straw beachcomber hat and some lovely black coral and silver jewellery. Happy and pleasantly tired, so that the evening meal in the open-sided dining-room was not the ordeal other meals had been since Mark Learmonth had arrived. And since she'd felt herself under his scrutiny from the other end of the dining-room—his sardonic scrutiny, perhaps.

Of course she hadn't been able to avoid Mark and the Waterfords entirely, but being always in the company of others and being so active had helped so much.

I'm winning, she told herself as she went to bed early and knew she would sleep.

The next evening was the once-weekly disco night, when all the equipment arrived on *Thunbibi* and after a fish barbecue everyone congregated in the bar, also an open-sided, thatched building with a deck out over the beach and open to the stars, and a dance-floor.

Philippa changed her mind several times but, in the end, went—her middle-aged English friends insisted and they'd got up a party of nine. An uneven number because of her, of course, but no one in the party seemed to be counting; and no one, least of all Philippa, appeared to be aware that the irritable young Englishman she'd overheard on the beach was. Or that he had decided to abandon his diving friends in the cause of evening things up or, more accurately, making a determined effort to get to know to Philippa, at least.

She even smiled at him briefly as he drew his

chair up next to her and introduced himself all round as Simon Bond—she'd put a face to his voice the day after she'd overheard the conversation on the beach then promptly forgotten all about it with Mark Learmonth to occupy her mind. Not to know that she had activated a burning resolve within this tall, dark, quite good-looking young man, or that she had become the object of a wager between him and his friends.

But for the first hour or so of the disco he behaved himself impeccably, and told her the names of all the stars and constellations above and pointed out the satellites as they curved through the heavens. And Philippa lay back in her chair on the deck sipping her wine and again gripped by that pleasant feeling of timelessness as they talked desultorily.

Then he asked her to dance.

She hesitated, but a sideways glance revealed Mark Learmonth at the next table and, despite herself, her heart jolted in her breast, so she stood up with a faint smile and walked away in her simple white sleeveless, square-necked dress and bare feet—no one ever wore shoes on Nakatcha—and her hair loose and vibrant on her shoulders, towards the flashing lights and music of the dance-floor.

Simon proved to be an active, imaginative partner and again, despite herself, Philippa found herself participating as the music got her in its grip. So much so that, after a few numbers, the dance-floor emptied as others gave way happily to their rhythm and expertise but stood around and clapped enthusiasm and encouragement.

It was Bob Marley and his 'Buffalo Soldier' that really caused her to let her hair down and let her skirt fly out as the crowd joined in and sang the choruses, and her feet flew and her body swayed to the rhythm. Then the last notes died away and there was a storm of applause and it seemed quite natural for Simon Bond to slide his arms around her and hold her close, both of them flushed and panting, and for another storm of applause to break out.

If she hadn't seen Mark Learmonth over Simon's shoulder, leaning against a pillar with a drink in his hands and a sceptical glint in his grey eyes as he stared straight into hers, the outcome to the disco night might have been quite different.

As it was, when Simon released her but kept hold of her hand, and suggested that they cool their feet in the sea, she acquiesced by simply turning her back on Mark and walking away with Simon.

He led her down to the water, out of sight of the bar and deck, and she hitched her dress up and they waded in and she laughed softly at the phosphorus that dissolved into trails of little stars caught in the water as she moved, and she looked up at her companion with her lips still curved into a smile.

There was a moment's pause, then Simon Bond said in a curiously tortured voice, 'Oh, God, you're the most exquisite thing I've ever seen!'

And he pulled her into his arms again and began to kiss her urgently.

To her dying day, Philippa knew she would find it hard to forgive herself for her lack of preparedness which, while it didn't last that long, lasted just long enough to further give Simon Bond the wrong impression, and to make what she did then unacceptable.

So that she was bruised and breathless when she finally got free of him, and angry. 'You have no right to think——' she started to say.

'No?' he drawled, interrupting her. 'Then you shouldn't have danced with me the way you did, lady. Or is Paul right, after all?'

'I danced to the music,' Philippa said raggedly. 'That's. . . Who is Paul?'

'My mate—as they say down your way, I believe. He reckons you're as cold as a maggot—you've got to be or you wouldn't be here on your own, consorting with the elderly and married couples only——'

'*Oh*. . .' Philippa stared at him with her breasts heaving, then she turned on her heel, stumbled out of the water, ran about twenty paces and straight into Mark Learmonth.

'Why, Philippa,' he murmured, fielding her effortlessly and steadying her with his hands about her waist, 'has your Romeo proved to be a philistine?' She moved and raised a hand, but he caught her wrist and said mildly, 'Now, now, Boadicea. I was merely an unwilling onlooker.'

'Or a willing eavesdropper,' Philippa said

through her teeth. 'Or some sort of unpleasant vulture?'

His teeth glinted white in the moonlight, in a lazy smile. 'Not even that. My rondavel happens to be on this path, two down, and I was on my way to bed. Would you care to join me for a nightcap on the beach?' He paused. 'We could discuss this traumatic turn of events and perhaps put it into a better perspective for you.'

Philippa's shoulders sagged suddenly. 'We?' she said bitterly, then, 'I doubt there is a better perspective for me, and you would have to be the last person who could find it for me. So I think you should pursue your original plan and I will also go to bed.'

He said softly, 'Alone?'

She stared up at him. 'If you're suggesting what I think you are, that's cheap and——'

'Despicable,' he said wryly. 'It actually—er—activated my sense of humour to think of us chastely pursuing the same plan in different beds, but then I do sometimes have an odd sense of humour, so I'm told. Very well,' he released her wrist, 'we will go back to Plan A—a nightcap on the beach. Do you drink Scotch?'

'I. . .'

Ten minutes later and not quite sure how it had happened, but suspecting an implacable will in a velvet glove that appeared to be more than a match for hers, Philippa sipped a fairly strong Scotch and water.

Mark had pulled up two white wooden loungers to the edge of the water and, apart from the distant music of the disco, they could have been a million miles from anywhere.

She sighed and lay back.

'Feeling better?'

She grimaced. 'Yes. And no. Perhaps I did lead him on, dancing like that, but these days when you hardly ever touch your partner. . .' She shrugged.

'It might have something to do with the way one moves.'

She glanced at him. 'Body language?'

His mouth quirked. 'Added to a body like yours.'

'So I told the whole world I was a. . .frustrated spinster,' she said wearily.

'Are you? But not exactly that,' he continued before she could say anything. 'I think you expressed a—perhaps unconscious—sensuality. I wouldn't worry too much about Simon Bond, however. He's lost a bet so that's galling him as well.'

Philippa froze. 'With a certain Paul, by any chance?' she asked arctically.

'Paul, young Karl and I can't remember the other one's name, but they're all together here on a diving holiday and it's a matter of great interest to them whether you are—beddable, who will be the one to achieve it, and whether it will be a worthwhile achievement. I suppose,' he looked at her quizzically, 'we're all wondering that. It's human nature,' he added softly.

'Be that as it may,' she said swiftly, 'are you telling me you actually stood by and—or did you even participate?' She stared at him with stormy eyes.

He laughed. 'No, I didn't. I *do* know you better than they do——'

'But not well enough to——' Philippa broke off with a disgusted sound and deliberately drank some Scotch. 'I despise the whole lot of you,' she said barely audibly but with considerable feeling.

'Be *that* as it may,' he said drily, 'we're not all really as despicable as you seem to think. If you could relax a little about it all, it might help.'

'I don't——' Philippa stopped and started again. 'I don't know how this came about, but if you've really decided for reasons best known to yourself to mount a "save Philippa Wright from *herself*" campaign, I'm not in need of it, as I keep telling you!'

'No?'

'No.'

'Then let's talk about something else,' he said quietly. 'Did you enjoy Male?'

Philippa laid her head back and gazed at the stars. 'I loved it. Have you enjoyed your diving so far?'

'Yes—although the current was so strong today it was rather exhausting. But yesterday we were lucky enough to see some Manta rays overhead. And of course it's a whole new world down there for Gary. You should try it. Hans, the diving instructor, is very good.'

Philippa shivered slightly.

'Does it really frighten you?' he asked.

'I guess it does,' she said slowly. 'Anyway, I've never been game to try it. There are some things you just know—aren't your forte.'

'Like love,' he said idly and held up his hand as Philippa tensed. 'Don't worry, I didn't relax you only to start needling you again—that just slipped out. Why don't you tell me about some of the things that are your forte? How you come to be such a good dancer, for example.'

Philippa subsided and stared at the stars. 'This will probably make you laugh, but at one stage in my life I desperately wanted to be a disco dancer.' She sipped her Scotch, and even when he smiled faintly couldn't rouse herself to antagonism. 'What was it with you?' she queried. 'A fireman?'

He grimaced. 'Perhaps when I was about three. No, I wanted to be a barrister, distinguished counsel, that kind of thing—until I realised it was the play-acting that appealed to me more than anything and that the sordid sifting through people's lives did not.'

Philippa lifted a hand and chuckled with genuine amusement.

He raised an eyebrow.

'Do you know, for the first time you've actually presented me with some ammunition, Mark Learmonth?' she said, still grinning. 'From the way you've pinned me in the dock and attempted to sift through my life, I have to say you should have stuck to your first choice!'

'Ah, but there was something about you, Philippa, that made it irresistible.

She put her empty glass on the sand and slid her hands beneath her hair to raise it and let the cool little breeze fan her neck. 'Was it because I didn't lie down in the aisle for you? That's Len Colefax, by the way,' she said, but rather half-heartedly because the Scotch or something seemed to have taken the edge off her animosity, or so she thought.

'Perhaps,' he said quietly.

Her hands tensed then she withdrew them and her hair sank like a cloud. 'That's ridiculous,' she said tartly.

'Is it? Why?'

'Because—you know it is. And I'm going to bed!' She rose and started to march up the beach.

He had no trouble catching her up. 'I can find my way, thank you,' she said coldly and pointedly.

'I'm sure you can but, belatedly, I'm taking up the responsibility of our acquaintanceship,' he said gravely. 'Your spurned suitor might be lurking in the bushes.'

'I'll kill you if you laugh at me again,' Philippa remarked as they walked side by side along the path. 'Nor do I need any help to cope with Simon Bond, if that's what you meant by "the responsibility of our acquaintanceship", which didn't deceive me for all its utterly pompous turn of phrase. What are you doing?' she demanded as he took her arm and stopped her a few feet from her rondavel veranda.

'Philippa Wright,' he murmured, turning her to face him, then just studying her meditatively.

'What?' She'd meant to say it defiantly but it came out sounding rather unsure. They were very close and he put his free hand on her other arm, above her elbow.

'You're working yourself into a frenzy over nothing,' he said deliberately. 'That's what. Goodnight.' He turned and walked away without a backward glance.

She hired a surf ski the next morning with the intention of paddling right round the island and observing the coral below the water. It was something she'd done before and it didn't take long to regain some proficiency with the double-bladed paddle, and she set off stroking quite smoothly over the glassy surface of the water that revealed the marvels below in all their glory.

It took her about an hour, with frequent admiring stops, but she couldn't deny she was tired and aware of muscles she'd forgotten she possessed when it was over. So she collected herself a long, cool drink from the bar and took it to her favourite patch of beach where a cotton-wood tree hung over to touch the water and provide deep, cool shade; and she lay back on her beach towel. And there she stayed for about an hour, taking the odd dip in the sea.

It was while she was doing this that she got buzzed by the Indian Navy—in a manner of speaking.

Most mornings a helicopter from the Indian warship in Male harbour did a tour of the islands, a relic from the coup days apparently, and she was lying in the shallows when she heard it approach and circle Nakatcha, saw it fly directly overheard low and heading towards Baros, then bank sharply and turn and come in even lower—directly towards her.

Her first reaction was to wave; then, as it came closer and lower, she sat up suddenly with a tremor of apprehension. But, at what seemed like the last moment to her, it banked again and flew off.

She heaved a relieved sigh and heard someone laugh softly behind her. A laugh she recognised without having to turn round—Mark Learmonth.

She did turn and she stared at him steadily for a moment then she said, 'That amused you?'

He was standing on the water's edge and he shrugged and waded in and sat down beside her. 'That was a considerable compliment, Philippa.' His grey eyes lingered on her white, one-piece swimsuit.

'Was it?' she replied tartly. 'I wish they'd let me know they weren't about to attack.'

He grinned and continued to observe her lazily. 'You know, I have to confess I'm still amazed at your transformation. And I suppose I also have to confess that I can see your point to an extent. All this,' he gestured with an idle sweep of his hand from her head to her toes, 'feminine perfection must be rather hard to handle. I mean you've even got the—I'm sure rather austere—Indian Navy into a bit of a twitter. You're the kind of girl who could probably create riots.'

Philippa closed her eyes against the sun. 'Am I supposed to take that as a compliment? Well, I'm sorry to say it doesn't quite strike me as one.'

But when she opened her eyes it was to see him looking completely unrepentant. 'I didn't actually think it would,' he murmured. 'Tell me, are you one of those militant feminists who honestly believe men's sincere admiration of them is a form of abuse?'

'If you're asking me, in other words, whether I enjoy being ogled, no, I don't, so perhaps I am. Tell *me* something, Mark, would you class yourself as an ogler?'

'Not so much an ogler,' he said thoughtfully, 'as an observer of the finer things of life. Have I ever ogled you?'

'I'd like to know what else one could call it in this particular instance,' she said acidly and jumped up and strode back to the beach, where she picked up her beach towel and wrapped herself in it defiantly and sat with her arms about her knees.

He followed and sat also, about two feet away, and when he spoke again it was in a different tone. 'I apologise. There appears to be something between us that brings out the worst in me. . .us, perhaps I should say us. I know I've mentioned this before but I'm doing so again because I've given the matter some thought in the interim, and it's occurred to me what the reason for this state of affairs might be.'

'Oh?' Philippa said coldly.

'Mmm. . .' he mused, looking not at her but down at the sand and a pattern he was drawing in it. Then he went on with a little shrug, 'Unless, of course, your period of spinstership has begun to get you down as it might any healthy young woman. For a moment there last night you did seem to melt into young Bond's arms.' He raised his grey gaze to hers.

Philippa opened her mouth, then buried her face in her knees suddenly to hide the blush she felt rising to her cheeks.

'Philippa?' he said after a long pause.

'That was sheer surprise,' she said crossly, looking up at last but straight ahead. 'He doesn't excite me in the slightest——'

'Something got you going,' he murmured.

'It was,' she retorted then rested her chin on her knees, 'the music, the night, the place, whatever,' she said wearily.

'A romantic impulse, the desire to allow your body and soul the freedom you deny it normally, something like that, you mean?'

'But not with Simon Bond,' she said tartly, then bit her lip and tried to retrieve things. 'Nor was I to know he was pursuing in earnest—if he was and not just protecting his pocket-money.'

'Oh, he was.'

'Look, could you tell me what all this is leading up to?' Philippa said impatiently. 'It's nearly lunchtime and, whatever else you like to believe of me, I do have a normal, healthy appetite!'

'Well, that's just what I'm trying to sort out,' he said placidly. 'How much of last night might have been your repressed hormones taking over and how much of it might have had to do with me.'

Philippa rounded on him, her eyes sparking green fire. 'You have the most incredible nerve,' she whispered.

'Have you said that to me before?' he queried meditatively. 'It seems to have a familiar ring.'

'How many times until you *believe* it, then?'

'I might be more believing when you stop saying it, Philippa. When you admit the real reason for your acute hostility towards me. And my desire to retaliate.' He shrugged. 'Let's be honest.'

She stared at him and felt the most extraordinary sensation, a feeling of nameless dread, a sensation she'd felt last night, she remembered, when he'd made that amazing admission to her, an admission that placed him more than ever in the ranks of her brother and father.

'I really don't know what you mean,' she said stiffly.

He raised an eyebrow. 'Don't? Or won't? Or perhaps you understand all too well, my Boadicea, but, just in case I've underestimated your powerful intelligence, I'll put it into words. Such an acute state of hostility between two people of the opposite sex generally has its roots in something else.'

She could only stare at him still with her lips parted, her green eyes wide, and her whole being suddenly and treacherously flooded with a mixture of shame and sensitivity to everything about him that disturbed and attracted her despite the arrogance and what she knew was about to come. . . She tore her gaze away and looked down at the pattern he'd drawn on the sand and his hands, but that was a mistake as it crossed her mind that she loved his hands—but how could she ever justify loving a man's hands when he was about to torment her even more than he'd ever done? She looked up defiantly.

'Do you understand what I'm saying, Philippa?' he said very quietly, but his grey eyes probed hers without mercy. And he went on, 'Speaking for myself, I now know it's true, however unlikely, but the fact remains—we may not like each other, Philippa, but we want each other. Wouldn't you agree?'

'No.' It came out sharply and quite definitely—and just a little too pat.

'You haven't even stopped to contemplate it,' he said unerringly. 'I find that strange. What are you denying, incidentally? That I don't feel the way I do, that you don't, or——?'

'If you feel that way *now,*' she said shortly, having taken steely hold of her resources, 'it's nothing but,' she gestured towards the horizon contemptuously, 'the same thing the Indian Navy is suffering from. Perhaps you should think twice before you come alone, in that sense, to these romantic tropical islands—perhaps you're getting dive-happy and should try another hobby——'

'Philippa,' he interrupted amusedly, 'you're working yourself into a frenzy again, my dear. I have to wonder why.'

'I am not,' she retorted. 'I'm merely pointing out that we may be suffering from the same syndrome, my suppressed hormones and your lack of a partner which this heavenly,' she gestured sardonically this time, 'romantic environment is playing upon—and please don't say one more word because I wouldn't believe anything else, and I am going to lunch!'

CHAPTER FIVE

LUNCH proved to be a tasteless experience and Philippa's afternoon siesta, once again, an unpleasant little cross-examination period because it struck her again, as it had on the beach and made her blush, that Mark was right. The music of the night before had betrayed her body and soul—at least it had been the catalyst that had betrayed his influence on her body and soul. But to believe that Mark Learmonth was after anything more than an interlude with a girl who had surprised him after refusing to keel over for him was not possible. Therefore, she told herself, I will admit nothing—except what I've already admitted, she thought with a sudden pang. Blame it all on my hormones, in other words! Not that I'm going to give him the opportunity to make me admit anything. . .

'How did this happen?' Philippa queried tautly as she helped Mark Learmonth launch a catamaran into the clear, sparkling Indian Ocean the next morning. The couple in charge of the water sports had organised a combined sailing and windsurfing expedition across to the twin islands of Boduhithi and Kudahithi north of Nakatcha. Philippa had put her name down to go on one of the catamarans, desperate for something to do and something to take her away from Mark Learmonth, who she'd hoped would be diving anyway. 'Did you engineer it?'

He shrugged and squinted up at the colourful sail. 'Not with any thought of rape or seduction in mind. I should imagine that would be a good way to end up in the drink. Have you ever sailed one of these?'

'Yes,' she said shortly then sighed. 'So I can handle the jib.'

'Welcome aboard, then,' he said with a faint wry smile.

They set out cautiously with the jetty to clear and the narrow channel through the reef to negotiate, then picked up a breeze and soon the little craft was flying through the water as they tacked and circled the group of windsurfers, and the sun shone on the deep, inky blue of the ocean and the silver spray cooled their faces—and it was impossible not to be invigorated and cleansed of most emotion.

It was also soon obvious that Mark Learmonth was an expert sailor, that he could drive the cat between two windsurfers with beautiful precision and turn it on the proverbial sixpence.

'Are we riding shotgun?' Philippa raised her voice to ask once.

He grinned. 'Some of the windsurfers aren't very experienced so, yes, it's handy to have the cats out. As a matter of fact,' he glanced around,

'I doubt if we'll make the islands—some of the others are also tiring.'

And Philippa saw Tom, the leader of the expedition, bring his cat round and call a rest.

So they circled gently while the windsurfers sat on their boards resting, and the water glittered and Philippa rested her back against a transom wire and lifted her face to the sun and the blue, blue sky, and the magic of being in these beautiful reef-studded waters only a few degrees north of the equator, west of India and Sri Lanka and east of Africa.

'What are you thinking?'

She opened her eyes and looked at Mark Learmonth, sitting towards the back of the little boat with the rudder stick in his hands, and the golden, lean length of him stretched out in a pair of colourful navy blue and red Bermuda shorts, and nothing else. With his hair windblown and streaked with salt and his grey eyes resting on her thoughtfully.

'It's hard to put into words,' she said truthfully. 'Perhaps I was indulging in a "the world is my oyster" kind of feeling. Africa over there,' she waved a hand, 'and. . . I don't really know,' she finished ruefully.

'Sounds as if you are a born traveller.'

She closed her eyes and said nothing but knew his gaze was still resting on her. She'd taken the precaution against the sun of putting a soft violet cotton blouse and white shorts over her silvery grey and white bikini, and tied the front ends of the blouse into a knot at her waist. And she knew her hair would be wind-tangled and that the sun-cream she'd smoothed all over her would be giving her skin an extra sheen. She also knew her nerve-ends were quivering beneath that grey scrutiny.

He said at length, 'Is there any reason for us not to get to know each other better, Philippa, if nothing else?'

'What would be the point?'

'To further explain, perhaps, the impact we have on each other?' he suggested.

'I think it might be better left unexplained.'

'Now that's an admission I thought you weren't prepared to make, Miss Wright,' he drawled. 'I congratulate you on deciding to be honest, even if belatedly.'

Philippa said something she normally didn't say and turned her head away from the glint of laughter in his eyes.

'I guess it was an admission that might have just slipped out, though,' he said philosophically then and added, 'It can happen to the best of us.'

She drew an irritated breath. 'Look, you did promise you weren't here to ruin my holiday. I——'

'Dear Philippa, look at me.'

She swung her head back defiantly, her greenish eyes angry and contemptuous.

'That was before,' he said softly, 'it occurred to me that you really were dying to make love to someone as you yourself admitted—and it might as well be me.' His eyes slid down to her breasts rising and falling beneath the violet blouse and the wisp of silk beneath, down to her long, bare legs then back to her mouth and finally her eyes.

'You. . .' How she had the quickness of mind to do it she never knew, but she was on her knees in a flash and she thrust out her hands with every intention of pushing him off the boat—and succeeded. The only thing that went wrong was that he took her with him, and as she toppled over into the water she saw his teeth flashing in a rueful grin.

Things were a little confused from then on but the ever watchful Tom zoomed in to help, and while she swallowed water and promised herself that she would curse Mark Learmonth to her dying day, he hauled himself back on board lithely, and leant down a hand to her, laughing still and at the same time conducting a conversation with Tom that she missed most of.

And she was panting with exertion, and dripping, when she finally lay on the trapeze and realised hazily that a change of plan had taken place. She sat up as Mark expertly took control of the jib rope as well as the main sail, turned the craft and sailed it away from the group and away from Nakatcha.

'What. . .where are we going?' she gasped, pushing her sodden hair off her face.

'We've been relieved of riding shotgun,' he said lightly. 'And seeing as you're so keen to—er—

swim, I thought I'd take you to a better spot for it.'

Philippa spluttered something incomprehensible then managed to say, 'No. Turn back.' And she looked back but it was to see that the whole of the little fleet was waving to them, and laughing and cheering. A deep blush burned her cheeks as she turned back and swore. 'Do they. . .did they. . .?'

He raised his eyebrows. 'Hear? I doubt it. I think they all assumed it was just a good-natured piece of horseplay and are happily unaware of the. . .dangerous currents that actually flow——' he paused '—I was going to say between us, but from you to me would be more accurate, don't you think?'

'No, I don't. You wouldn't be carting me off God knows where——' She stopped abruptly.

'You could be right,' he said serenely. 'By the way, you wouldn't get away with it a second time, Boadicea,' he added idly. 'So you might as well just accept that, for some things, you have to pay.'

A tremor ran down Philippa's spine because, although his words were light and he looked perfectly relaxed and still faintly amused, she'd also seen that laid-back glint in his eyes before and knew it spelt danger. She hunched her shoulders and stared out to sea, which was whichever way she looked except one. And asked herself miserably what she thought might have possessed her.

They sailed in silence for about fifteen minutes.

The breeze had freshened so they were singing along and were almost upon it before Philippa roused from her morbid reverie and saw the arc of golden sand ahead.

That was all it was, a curve of beach rising from the water as they sometimes did in these atolls, with no trees or plant life and almost blinding in their golden radiance and trim of white lace ripples. A perfect spot for a swim, she thought desolately. A perfectly beautiful and private spot for anything. But, because she couldn't think of anything else to do, she helped bring the catamaran in, then jumped off into the shallows, turned it into the wind and helped Mark beach it. Then she looked around and, with a suppressed sigh, took her shorts off but didn't worry about her wet blouse, and went for a swim.

He didn't bother her in the water but swam himself, lay in the shallows for a while, then opened the small cool-box on the cat and produced two cans of soft drink.

Philippa was also lying in the shallows some way away, but she could see what he was doing and she could hear the ring-pull of the can releasing and could feel her throat muscles contract with thirst. He made no move to bring her a drink.

She stood up and wondered if he could detect the way her mind was working, that she was doing a mental countdown—nine, ten, out. . . Could tell that her nerves were taut and close to breaking-point.

But she forced herself to stroll towards the

catamaran and to sink down beside it in the water and in the shade of the sail as he was, and to say lightly, 'Thirst is a powerful master. I gather I'm expected to make some reparation for my sins or pay some forfeit. We might as well get it over with.' And the gaze she bestowed on him, by an enormous effort of will, was clear and green.

His lips twisted and he handed her a can. 'What did you have in mind?'

She opened the can and took a long, thirsty draught. Then she said flatly, 'The obvious—some form of physical submission during which you show me how right you are about me and I dissolve into a state of mindless desire and feminine helplessness. Can I say one thing before we begin, though?'

'I'd be most amazed if you didn't,' he murmured.

She stared at him then said abruptly, 'Have you ever loved anyone?'

He laid his head back against the cat. 'If you mean—sufficiently loved anyone to want to *plunge* into marriage with them, the answer is obviously no. Or were you hoping I had some great, unrequited love in my life?'

'So you're not. . .' She stopped. So you're not thinking of marrying someone 'as a matter of fact', she'd been about to say, but that was an admission of supreme interest, wasn't it? she thought. 'It might help to know that at least you believed in it,' she said instead and bit her lip.

He laughed softly. 'Might it? Help who? You?'

'*You're* the one who is insisting we. . .affect each other,' she said through her teeth. 'I just wondered how you saw. . .what. . .oh, hell——'

'What future there would be for an affair with me? Then I'll tell you what I believe—that it does exist—love—but it's a very rare thing.'

'So your philosophy is not to knock yourself about too much or disorganise your life trying to find it, and to enjoy yourself none the less.' She couldn't hide the bitterness in her voice.

He shrugged. 'Can one go looking for it?'

'Perhaps not, but one can passively resist it, if that's the way one is.'

'Now that,' he said thoughtfully, 'is something that might apply to you, Philippa. Well, not the passive bit.' His eyes glinted with amusement.

Philippa made a disgusted sound.

'As for me,' he continued lazily and raked a hand through his wet hair, 'what can I tell you to set your mind at rest? That I don't go about it quite so cold-bloodedly as you seem to imagine and I don't think any of the women I've slept with during my long, uninterested——' he glanced at her mockingly '—career have actually regretted it, much as I know it will make your blood boil to hear it——'

'No, poor souls,' she broke in. 'Just that they failed to pin you down. Little did they know it but they were lucky really. What would it take to pin you down, I wonder?'

He was silent for a long time, his grey gaze

resting on her enigmatically. Then he said, 'You *do* have a lot of difficult hang-ups, Philippa.'

She felt herself colour and knew she'd made a tactical error—the whole conversation had been a mistake, it had still been an admission of interest, also an admission which had allowed him to see her prejudices, thus weakening her case. . .

'All right,' she said abruptly. 'That's all I wanted to say.' But there was a challenge in her straight green gaze.

'Somehow I don't believe that, *but*,' he said gravely, 'if you're inviting me now to go ahead and extract a physical forfeit—you got it wrong. All I meant was that you would have no choice about spending a little more time in my company. Anything else would be slightly ridiculous and adolescent, don't you think?'

It was just as well she got her tongue out of the way in time otherwise she'd have bitten it in half, Philippa realised, but a spark of articulacy and a spark of pure fighting spirit came to her aid as she stood up gracefully and stared down at him, and said with a cool smile, 'I hoped you'd see it that way, Mr Learmonth. I——'

She got no further as he demonstrated that he could move as quickly as she had earlier and, although she did half turn, his arms closed around her and he pulled her down to her knees beside him in the water and with deliberate efficiency ripped her blouse apart, released her bikini top unerringly then held her with one arm about her waist like a steel bar and her wrist in his other hand.

'Perhaps this is how you really like it, Miss Wright,' he drawled through his teeth. 'Is that what all your barbed taunts are about—a goad? You won't mind, then,' he scanned her appalled eyes through half-closed lids, 'if I oblige?'

He lowered her wrist and trapped it behind her back with her other one and with his free hand cupped her head, and claimed her lips with his.

It was about as defiling, the way he kissed her, as anything she could think of. A practised invasion of her mouth but with no tenderness, a sensuous possession that was also brutal, and the only difference from the little scenario she had so foolishly drawn was that while it did make her feel helpless and as if her bones had turned to water, it was not from desire but because of his strength that she couldn't fight and the implicit, savage mockery of it all.

Nor did it end there. He raised his mouth from hers as last and, while she gasped for breath, he held her away from him so that he could, with indifferent appreciation, leisurely inspect her breasts that had been crushed against him, the curve of her waist and hips until they met the grey and white of her bikini bottom, and her thighs as she knelt still in the circle of his arms. Then he looked up again and their eyes clashed and she shivered at what she saw.

But she was unable to tear her gaze away and unable to hide the chaos of her soul in her eyes—

the guilt: had she goaded him into it? And, incredibly, where there had been shock and defilement, now there was a sudden contracting of all her senses, a humming through the air between them that almost had the power to make her raise her hand and touch him, her fingertips actually tingling as she stared into those grey eyes and imagined the feel of his smooth tanned shoulders beneath her hands, the contrasting roughness of the hairs on his chest. . . And then the imagined delight of kissing him willingly, her lips opening eagerly beneath his, her breasts straining against him instead of being crushed, the wayward wonder of lying with him in these lapping shallows, naked and unashamed.

But what he said killed it all.

'There's a thousand US dollar fine for going topless in these parts, Philippa.' And he released her indifferently.

She sank on to her heels and her wet hair fell foward to shadow her face as she pulled the edges of her blouse together and looked around desperately for her bikini top. They were still close to each other although he was sitting in the water now, and he reached behind him and picked it up and handed it to her.

She dropped it and plunged her hand into the water that was lapping her thighs to retrieve it, then her other hand as a little surge of the tide took it away, and the violet blouse fell open again and her breasts, pale and full and soft, swung loose and free as she turned her body frantically as the errant tide carried it past her.

He moved then, reaching round her and grabbing it and, this time, picked up her hand, put it into it and closed her fingers about it. He also said abruptly, 'There's no one to see us, don't panic.'

She put a hand to her brow shakily then pulled her blouse together again awkwardly.

'Philippa?'

It was an age before she could force herself to meet that grey gaze, but less because she was panic-stricken about being caught topless in this Islamic land and much more to do with what she'd see in his eyes now.

But, when she looked up at last, the mockery had been replaced by a brooding sombreness, then he swore beneath his breath and said with a curious roughness that didn't seem directed at her so much as himself. 'Put it on—if it's any consolation, I don't feel too good about myself right now.'

'I. . .' Her voice caught in her throat. 'If I asked for it in any way——'

'You didn't enjoy it, that much was obvious. Well,' he lifted his shoulders, 'not——' But he stopped and his grey gaze sharpened on something over her shoulder, then he was up on his knees, swearing again but this time quite audibly, causing her to look round in alarm and wonder if she *had* been caught virtually topless although there was not a boat or a speck of humanity in sight, she saw, and it was a moment before she took in what he had seen.

A rain squall darkening the horizon with angled pencil lines to the water, and, she realised from the way the wind was blowing, they were directly in its path.

'Oh. . .'

'I think we can outrun it,' he said tersely. 'The wind is blowing towards Nakatcha too—unless you feel like riding it out here?'

'N-no,' she stammered. 'There's no cover, but——'

'Don't worry, I won't drown you,' he said and, from the way he got the cat back into the water and his purposeful but never exaggerated movements and the cool, calculating look of him, she believed him.

Nevertheless it was a close-run thing as she clung to the little craft and they ploughed through the swell. She left the handling of the jib to him and they both wore the lifejackets that had been tied to the trapeze; he'd instructed her to worry about one thing only—staying on board.

It also turned out to be—God knew how, she thought once—one of the most exciting things she'd ever done, perhaps because she couldn't doubt his mastery of the boat and the wind, perhaps because, above all else, she couldn't doubt now that Mark Learmonth was supremely capable in all he undertook—even the wrecking of me, she thought with a little pang.

There was an anxious reception committee

awaiting them on the beach as the first raindrops fell at about the same time as they sailed through the channel in the reef.

'I'll no doubt get a lecture from Tom over this,' Mark observed wryly and raised his voice as the rain fell more heavily. 'This is not the first time today that we've looked like drowned rats.'

'No,' she replied quietly with her eyes on the beach. 'High comedy and high drama—at least they all got home safely. I wouldn't have liked to be out on a windsurfer in this.'

'Tom would have spotted it long before I did and shepherded his flock home in plenty of time—but I don't suppose that's the high drama you meant.'

'No, although I actually enjoyed the last bit,' she said carefully then went on determindedly but with a slight tremor in her voice, 'I think we should leave it at that.'

'I don't see how we can.' He tacked round the jetty.

But Philippa knew her nerves could stand no more and she looked at him desperately as they slid towards the beach. '*Please*. . .just let me go.' She held her breath.

His grey gaze lingered on her anguished eyes, then he shrugged slightly and said coolly, 'If that's what you want. Can you cleat the jib rope? Oh, hell,' he added as the crowd on the beach erupted into a storm of applause.

CHAPTER SIX

ONE disadvantage of being on an island, especially an island as small as Nakatcha, was that no man could be an island unto himself—and no woman.

Nor did the weather conspire with Philippa in any way. The rain squall passed, the sun shone from a cloudless sky and preparations for Lobster Night, a specially festive dinner held each week, went inexorably ahead and by dusk the tables were set up on the beach.

She had also tentatively approached the management—and in the process pained them to think that she might not be enjoying her holiday—to enquire how simple it would be to cut it short. Only to discover it would not be in the least simple. Singapore Airlines flights from Male to Singapore, which originated in Europe anyway, proved to be fully booked for the next couple of days. There were other flights, of course, they told her, and no doubt in the case of a genuine emergency something could be arranged, but she was on a Singapore Airlines package subject to certain conditions, the breaking of which could prove very costly, if nothing else.

She returned to her rondavel as the sun set,

defeated and dispirited, ordering coffee from the dining-room on the way.

She was sitting cross-legged on her bed, in a pair of plum shorts and a sleeveless, scoop-necked silky cream top, when the coffee arrived—or what she thought was the coffee, but on opening the door discovered it was Mark Learmonth who had knocked, and that the waiter with the coffee was only paces behind him, thereby making it impossible to shut the door in his face. So the coffee came in and so did he as she signed the inevitable chit.

And she couldn't help herself from saying ironically, 'Would *you* like a cup? I'm sure we could order another.'

'Thank you,' he murmured, and the waiter scurried away to oblige.

Mark closed the door and leant his shoulders back against it, and observed her meditatively. He was dressed, although casually, for dinner in a white shirt and blue cotton trousers, and his brown hair was brushed and tidy, and they stared at each other in the dimness for a moment until she felt the bare skin of her neck and throat beginning to flush.

She walked away from him and began, 'I don't know what you've come to say, but——'

'They tell me you want to leave,' he broke in.

Philippa stopped pacing and swung round with a gasp. 'How dare they? It's got nothing to do with anyone else, least of all *you*.'

'That's debatable,' he said drily. 'But they mentioned it to me because they're nice people, they don't like to think of you being unhappy here for no apparent reason, and because,' he lifted his shoulders, 'I happened to walk into the office only minutes after you'd left to get something from my safety deposit and they were still discussing it. And,' his eyes held hers, 'furthermore, because nothing that happens on this island escapes them, they knew we were together today, we're also both Australians and they felt I might share their concern.'

'And their speculation, no doubt,' she said tautly. 'About this strange, lone female who has descended on them.'

'I don't know about that kind of speculation—they're certainly far too polite to indulge in it with a fellow guest—but it has to be a matter of record now, between us, that there are some things I find very strange about you, Philippa, and before that raises your hackles further—you obviously have the same problem with me.'

The second cup and another pot of coffee arrived before she could reply, not that one sprang immediately to mind. So she poured the coffee, handed him a cup and with a shrug pointed to a chair. She took her own to the bed.

And she stirred it with her head bent then straightened and said reluctantly, 'What you find strange is really only this: that I won't fall into your arms willingly—even,' she said bitterly, 'when you'd probably have been horrified if I had. But I can't blame you for wondering whether I am a. . .certain type of neurotic or obsessional person after this morning. I don't think I am.' She paused then looked across the room at him. 'But yes, I am suspicious of you, Mark, and with reason. Not only for the things you've said and the unpleasant things you've implied about me but,' she hesitated, 'because I'm damn sure I'm only a challenge to you. Don't forget you told me yourself you were going to use your holiday to inject some enthusiasm into yourself, which was as good as saying you were jaded and all the rest of it. *That's* probably only why I ever intrigued you in the first place, and when you discovered I wasn't such a frump as I appeared, well, bingo.' She shrugged.

'Bingo again?' A cool smile twisted his lips. 'All right, let's assume you're right for a moment, but what about you?'

He was sitting in the cane chair with his arms resting spread out on its curved arms, one leg crossed so his ankle rested on his knee, and again he appeared quite relaxed and—yes, she thought with swift fury, aloof, damn him! While I'm wriggling around like some puzzling specimen under a microscope. . .

'Because this morning,' he continued thoughtfully, 'has had some curious consequences. *I* did what I did because I did think you were goading me into it at the time. I'd also been shoved off the back of a catamaran and. . .well, the heat of the moment got to me, you might say—even a point of male pride.' He smiled faintly but it was a dry, unamused smile. 'But if your taunts about my uninterested way with women are true, don't you think that by now I would have put you into a too hard, not to mention dangerously explosive basket?'

Philippa had to grimace but she said with some satire, 'How long is it since anyone said no to you, Mark?'

'Ah,' he drawled, 'but did you really say no this morning, Philippa? I know you hated the way I kissed you but you didn't retaliate—indeed you were quite stunned, but then, for a while, longing for better treatment. So how are we going to handle that?'

Philippa stared at him, her face a pale oval, her lips parted.

'You're not even going to admit that?' he said very softly.

'I. . .' She licked her lips and turned away convulsively, knocking her cup off the bedside table.

It bounced harmlessly but splashed tepid coffee over her legs. She muttered something incomprehensible and didn't realise he'd risen swiftly until he was standing over her with a towel in his hands. He knelt down beside her, wiped her legs and blotted up the puddle on the floor, restored her cup to the table then stayed kneeling beside her, looking into her eyes narrowly and interrogatively.

Philippa drew a shaky breath. He was so close she could breathe in the heady masculine essence of him and see the fine lines beside his eyes and bracketing his mouth; she could feel a primitive answering heat beneath the surface of her skin and she wondered if she could blame herself for losing control and simply saying—I do want you, let's forget about everything else. . .

'N-no,' she said raggedly. 'I'm not admitting anything. I've tried to explain because I felt——' she cleared her throat and went on huskily '—that I owed you one for this morning——'

'In point of fact you've explained nothing that I didn't already know.'

'Well, then, all you have to do now is accept it. . .'

'Accept what? That although an attraction does exist between us, you can't forget or forgive the insults I—*we*, to be precise, traded when we didn't realise or want to admit it could exist? To my mind that's childish, Philippa.'

She stared at him, her face pale and her eyes dark. 'Then you'd better accept this, Mark: I don't go in for casual relationships, I don't want to be any man's mistress, but least of all yours, and nothing you can say will make me change my mind.'

The silence was tension-charged and he prolonged it deliberately before he draped the towel over her knees and stood up. 'Do you know something, Philippa?' He looked down at her reflectively. 'You'd be much better off as my mistress than anyone else's. At least I understand you and I have some idea of your father's and your brother's role in making you like this—it wasn't that hard to work out,' he said at the sudden flash in her eyes. 'But one day all that repressed sensuality is going to break out, my dear, and make your life hell if the wrong man, or one who doesn't understand, gets in the way of it.'

'If anything,' she whispered, 'could be less calculated to make me change my mind, what you've just said is it.'

'But then you've always had an aversion to the truth, Philippa.' He pushed his hands into his pockets with a shrug. 'So be it. We'll keep the battle lines drawn——'

'It's *not* a battle!'

'No?' He looked down at her mockingly. 'What would you call it?'

'I. . .' But she couldn't speak further.

He smiled faintly. 'I'll see you at dinner—if you're game to come.' And he left.

She went.

Mainly because her options were limited to either simply skulking in her room and thereby causing further speculation, or concocting some plausible excuse when there was none. But she took a brightly vague mood with her like a coat of armour.

The tables on the beach were decorated with bougainvillaea blossoms, the wine was wrapped in broad green leaves in silver coolers, the stars were splashed across the night sky—and the Waterfords were in a festive mood, although once again Philippa thought she detected that reserve in Julia's eyes when she arrived.

As for Mark Learmonth, his grey eyes skimmed her loose, filmy, floating amber dress, the brave yellow cotton-wood flower in her hair—and they were as detached as they'd ever been.

The lobsters were small but delicious and the wine flowed freely. Then, fortunately when the meal was finished, the weather turned capricious again in the form of a rising wind and they removed to the bar, the matchstick blinds were rolled down, and it was bright and cheerful and cosy as the rain started.

The party spirit kept going but with a difference. Somehow Mark included her in his circle and for some reason his eyes were no longer so indifferent. Not that he paid that particular, special attention to her denoting anything lover-like between them, but he skilfully drew her into the conversation and the gaiety; and perhaps because her mental processes had been exhausted by her inner turmoil and the battering he had given it, she found she had the will to do nothing but go along, in a quiet way, with it. She found she couldn't even censor the treacherous thoughts that came as she watched him. The realisation was that she was seeing another side of Mark Learmonth, the humorous, laid-back side of his personality that was so likeable and not in the least self-important, and that, although it was laid-back, didn't hide a vitality and an intelligence that was fascinating.

She even thought once, a little numbly, that she could see why Ray had been so impressed.

But there were two consequences to her inclusion in the Learmonth-Waterford party, one she saw and one she missed. There could be no mistaking Julia Waterford's reserve this time—does she honestly believe I'm after her husband, Philippa thought with impatience, or that he's after me? Apart from one invitation to join them for dinner which was just a friendly gesture, I'm sure, he's made no *sign* and neither have I—God help me.

What she missed were Simon Bond's occasional dark looks that beamed her way, but by midnight, when the storm had abated, even her tired submission gave out and she knew she couldn't go on any longer. Perhaps it showed in her face because when she stood up to excuse herself Mark made no protest, although he did get up politely and walk to the steps with her.

She said with an effort. 'Thank you—for a nice night. I can get back to my rondavel alone—don't break up the party.'

'I wasn't going to,' he said quietly. 'You look so tired.'

'I am,' she admitted.

He had his back to everyone and he lifted a hand and touched her face lightly. 'Sorry. I didn't mean things to turn out quite as brutally as they did. Tomorrow I'll try and make amends. Goodnight, Philippa.' Her eyes widened but he smiled unexpectedly. 'Go to bed. I have no devious plans to—take advantage of you.'

She went straight to bed and fell asleep easily—only to wake a couple of hours later with a terrible feeling of panic in her heart and the knowledge that she was lodged somewhere between India and Africa and it was no longer romantic or anything but lonelier than she'd ever been.

She lay frozen under this burden for an age, trying to calm herself, trying to tell herself that she *was* at a dangerous age biologically and that possessing brains didn't automatically exempt one from those natural urges—a mate, a shared hearth, children, plans, the earthy pleasures of life—and she was right to protect herself against a man who, for all his attraction, was an unlikely one to give them to her. It still all came back to—and how could she doubt it?—the fact that she was more of a diversion to him than anything else. And so her mind went round in circles until she got up and roamed the room, feeling stifled and frightened.

Then she wrapped a sarong about her and stepped outside into the gentle rain.

The air was warm and humid after the air-conditioning and the beach was deserted. She stood on it for a long time. And the rain wet through her sarong and trickled down her face and she breathed deeply and deliberately—but the tears she was desperately trying to avoid came, to mingle saltily with the rain on her lips. And were brought on, she knew, by the thought that it would be so easy to hope he could be the right man for her, to surrender her will to his as she'd never done in her life—but what were the odds that she wouldn't end up like Jessica or her own mother—hopelessly in love with a man despite everything?

The only signs of the storm next morning, Philippa discovered, were some fallen palm fronds and a tide-mark of twigs and flotsam on the beach.

The signs of her personal storm were more evident, in fact, she thought, as she studied her face in the mirror after breakfast. Slight dark shadows beneath her eyes, definite marks of strain about her mouth and an indecisiveness in her manner.

The Waterfords and Mark had not been in the dining-room as she'd breakfasted but that was because they'd gone on an early dive, so she'd sat with her English friends and hoped that her tightened nerves were not as evident as they felt.

Now she turned away from the mirror, picked up a book and her beach towel and decided to read on the beach.

But she couldn't concentrate on anything, she found, excepting the dainty little ghost crabs that had been trapped by her stillness into believing she wasn't there. And for a little while she watched, fascinated as they waited at the water's edge until a ripple almost reached them then scurried away, on tiptoes if they mistimed it.

Then she sighed and stared at nothing in particular and thought with a sudden pang of remembrance—how could she have forgotten?—that she only had about a week left on Nakatcha. What do I mean, *only*? she asked herself immediately and bitterly.

The hot morning hours dragged but, well before lunchtime, she knew she couldn't face another stint in the dining-room, nor did she have any appetite, so she went back to her rondavel, closed the curtains and lay down wearily. Surprisingly, or perhaps not so, she fell deeply asleep for hours. And that was how she came to miss all the drama. . .

She was sitting in the coffee-shop, making up for her missed lunch with a cup of tea, when she became aware of a discernible difference in the air. People were talking to each other excitedly, a large group was gathered on the bar deck, and, looking the other way, she could see the reception area facing the jetty and that all the office staff were grouped in the walkway staring out to sea and talking. For some reason peaceful, sleepy Nakatcha was buzzing, she thought, and immediately tensed. Had there been another coup attempt?

It was Ali, in his broken English, who told her as he served her tea.

'Not coup,' he said with his toothy grin. 'Diving accident.'

'Di. . .' Philippa felt the colour drain from her face. 'Who. . .?'

'Mr Learmonth and Mr Bond. Mr Bond have some trouble with his equipment and Mr Learmonth stay down with Hans to help him. Both need decompression now for the bends,' Ali said with vigorous hand gestures. 'Hans reckon Mr Bond was taking stupid risk and got himself caught up in the coral and that's how he damaged equipment. I don't think,' Ali said thoughtfully, 'Mr Bond like Mr Learmonth and maybe he was showing off.'

Philippa's mouth dropped open. 'Why?' she said hoarsely.

'Why not like?' Ali stared at her then looked away vaguely. 'Who knows? I made you some little salad sandwiches, Miss Wright, you didn't have lunch,' he added reproachfully.

'Ali—thank you,' Philippa said confusedly. 'But will they be all right?' she asked desperately.

Ali shrugged his shoulders. 'I reckon so. Flying Swiss Ambulance Service pick 'em up and they're pretty damn good.'

'Where is the nearest decompression chamber?'

'Thuru—not far.'

It wasn't, Philippa knew. About an hour by dhoni from Nakatcha on the way to Male. 'Is Mr or Mrs Waterford with him?' she asked.

'All the Waterfords,' Ali said expansively. 'They go by speedboat; but you speak to Hans, he tell you everything.'

Hans was still looking grim and exhausted when she found him, but he allayed some of her fears—and deepened her worst suspicions.

'The word is that they'll both be all right but obviously out of action for a couple of days——'

'Are you *sure*?'

'*Ja*,' he said wearily. 'We just got a report by radio. It was Simon's own fault. He disobeyed my instructions, he left the group and from the exchange they had just before we dived, I think he was trying to prove he was as good if not a better diver than Mark.' He shrugged. 'There was obviously some animosity between them, but if I hadn't had Mark with me, Simon would have. . .' He shrugged again.

Philippa searched his face but Hans was not as easy to read as Ali, yet it was just that shuttered look she saw in his eyes that told her what she had suspected.

Suspected too late, she thought drearily as she walked away. The animosity was over me and the whole island knew it, except me.

She stopped abruptly then changed direction and walked towards the office.

And there, her humiliation was complete, she discovered, when she explained she still wanted to cut her holiday short. Because this time they got her a seat on the Singapore Airlines flight the next day and didn't really attempt to coax her to stay.

The morning she left Nakatcha was the most beautiful of all. The sea was pale and pearly for the first hour beneath a light wreathing of clouds and haze, and the flying fish leapt and dolphins frolicked. Then the haze lifted and the sun shone and the colours of the water came alive, the deep inky blue patterned with patches of turquoise and gold where the reef rose from the depths. And *Thunbibi* took her steadily towards Hulule Airport.

CHAPTER SEVEN

'THE Maldives! What made you choose to go there? And what were they like?'

'They were lovely, yes, well worth a visit and. . .'

If I have to describe the Maldives just once more I'll scream, Philippa thought, as she stood in the chaos of her parents' living-room on Christmas night, surrounded by her parents, an unusually subdued Ray—was he actually missing Jessica? she wondered—and friends. Christmas afternoon and evenings were traditionally for the Wrights, a time when friends popped in to exchange compliments of the season. In fact the whole week between Christmas and New Year was the same, and Philippa had unwisely allowed herself to be persuaded to spend it at home, but the alternative had been to spend it alone, she thought with a sigh, and on the whole that would be worse, so, take a deep breath, here comes someone else to ask me about the Maldives. . .

On the evening of New Year's Day, she let herself into her flat with a sigh of relief then ran to answer the phone, letting the door swing closed behind her. But it was only her lonely landlady downstairs, welcoming her back.

Philippa dealt with her curiosity gently, thankful that she hadn't come for a chat in person but sorry for her in a new way.

Then she had a shower because it was a hot, humid night in best Brisbane high summer fashion and, unlike in Nakatcha, she didn't have the benefit of air-conditioning. And she walked out of the bathroom wearing only a pair of briefs and opened a drawer to find a cotton nightshirt, and found instead a sarong she'd bought in Male.

She picked it up and held it in her hands and closed her eyes, and sniffed, for it had a very faint unmistakable smell and she'd discovered that everything she'd bought in Male had it. Not offensive but slightly musty, as if it had lain on its shelf in that little rickety upstairs shop where she'd bought it for years; a scent, moreover, that evoked so vividly the dusty streets of that little capital, the red betel-nut stains on the sand, the odd conglomeration of goods in some of the shops—washing-machines and sharks' teeth, dusty bottles of western shampoo. . . The waterfront alive with jostling *dhonis*, coconuts. . . Mark.

Tears pricked her eyelids and her lashes were wet as she sat down on the bed with the sarong in her hands, then swung her legs up and leant her head against the headboard, the sarong still bunched in her lap, and sweat dewing her brow and trickling down behind her ears and between her breasts as if she'd never taken a shower or might as well not have bothered in the heat of this night. And the despair because she couldn't forget him, and the loneliness. But what was there to remember? she asked herself as she had so many times. An awesome conflict of wills—yes, but to remember that doesn't alter this eerie sense of *loss*. A sense of irony because, now you've turned your back on him, the urge to know him is greater than ever, it's like a thorn in your mind and your flesh. . .

The doorbell rang and she got up and wrapped the sarong round her, not caring who it was but grateful for anything to relieve her loneliness. Then she hesitated halfway to the door as the bell rang again, and knew that no one could help her and she wouldn't be answering, but the decision was taken out of her hands—the door swung open and it was Mark.

Her mouth dropped open and she blinked rapidly but it *was* him, in grey denims and a black shirt, with his thick, smooth hair falling across his forehead and his Maldivian tan highlighting his grey eyes.

'How. . .?' she managed to say incredulously.

He held up his hand with her keys in it. 'I thought you must be home—these were in the door. Not a very wise practice, Philippa.'

She closed her eyes briefly, remembering how she'd let the door close as she ran to answer the phone, forgetting about her keys. 'Obviously not,' she whispered. 'But. . .*why*?' She searched his face tormentedly.

He was silent but his eyes mocked her, then he

said, 'I think you know that as well as I do, and running away wasn't the answer.'

'I didn't *run away*——'

'No? You could have fooled me,' he said evenly.

'But you. . .you. . .' The words stuck in her throat.

'What I tried to do was make it obvious, that last night, that I regretted some things and would like to make amends.'

'Well, what you overlooked was that I wasn't prepared to accept you regret,' she said bitterly. 'Nor was I prepared to stay and become the object of speculation and gossip and be fought over like a bitch on heat!'

'Philippa,' he said harshly, 'the fact that Simon Bond was a rash fool has nothing to do with this. Even if he did think I was succeeding where he'd failed——' he sent her a cutting pure grey glance '—little to know how wrong he was—but even if he did think that, it's no cause to endanger lives on the strength that you danced with him once. It's also no cause to blame me for what happened—it's only an excuse.'

She laughed hollowly then put a hand to her mouth and turned away. 'How did you find me?'

'I looked in the telephone book.'

'Of course!' She swung back and stared at him, trying to find something cutting to say in return, but then she heard herself saying involuntarily, 'Are you really all right? I mean,' she added hastily, 'No after-effects?'

He put her keys on the table and came towards her. 'None—from the dive. How are you?'

It was said soberly and he stopped right beside her so she had to tilt her head to look up into his eyes and she trembled at what she saw in them—the knowledge of exactly how she was. Her shoulders slumped and she took an unsteady breath.

'Tell me, Philippa.' He gazed down at her naked face.

She said with reluctant honesty, 'Isn't that like bringing on the rack, Mark? I should have thought it was obvious,' she finished barely audibly.

'Is it? Does that mean you regret running away like that—or whatever it was?' he said drily. 'That it's brought you no—comfort?'

Her lashes fluttered down then up and a nerve flickered in her jawline because she didn't know any more how she could go on fighting him. 'I don't regret leaving Nakatcha,' she said huskily. 'I do regret,' she paused and shrugged, 'feeling this way about you, because I don't know what it is I *really* feel and even less what you really feel, but no, it hasn't brought me much comfort.'

'Then would you say that, whatever else we might not know—staying away from each other is a kind of hell?' He stared into her greenish eyes that were partly bleakly honest, partly defiant. 'It has been for me, Philippa. That's why I'm here.'

Her lips parted and her breath caught in her throat as their gazes clashed and held, because the image of him printed in her mind since she'd left

Nakatcha had not lied as one part of her had secretly hoped, had not been inflated by a romantic, tropical island and all the trappings of moonlight, et cetera. And because nothing altered the way this man affected her, not the indifference he could assume, the austerity that was sometimes there and the opposite—an experience with women he didn't trouble to deny. Nothing changed the impact of those grey eyes and beautiful hands, his tall, discreetly strong body or the urge to know him, to match her mind to his. Yet something has changed, she thought confusedly. Whatever his need for her would be in the long term, however it would drown her will, she couldn't deny that it was there *now*—as much as hers was.

She moved her hands restlessly. 'We might always only hurt each other.'

'Perhaps we could heal each other,' he said sombrely and put his fingers on her chin, tilting it up and forcing her to stare into his eyes again until the rhythm of her breathing altered and she knew she was drowning in his closeness.

She tried to make one last-ditch effort. She tried to say something, but forgot almost immediately what it was as his fingers wandered down her throat and every nerve-ending in her body came alive. She forgot everything as her Male sarong fell open and slithered to the floor and only his intent grey gaze on her pale, pink-tipped breasts caused her nipples to unfurl.

He didn't touch them. Instead, he circled her

waist with his hands and looked into her eyes—which said all there was to say for her. Only then did he gather her yearning body close to him.

He made love to her as she'd known he would, as he did everything, expertly and sometimes mercilessly, so that her desire reached heights she'd never known and hadn't believed in, heights that seemed impossible to sustain, but sustain them he did, until she was pleading and aware of nothing but him and his mastery of her body. Yet the conclusion he finally brought to them was her victory as much as his, and he lay in her arms as helpless as she was beneath the pleasure and fulfilment that swept them both.

They drifted into an exhausted sleep without saying a word—there seemed no words to say and she woke hours later still with nothing to say but the memory of their lovemaking as vivid in her mind as if it had just happened. She moved cautiously at last and ran her hands slowly down her body. Then she sat up abruptly and stared around with the sheet clutched to her breasts. The very first flush of daylight was lightening the darkness and she said the first thing that came to mind. 'I have to go to work. . .'

Mark moved beside her and she turned convulsively to stare down at him, to see that he was grinning lazily, and he reached up and prised the sheet from her fingers and pulled her back down beside him.

'No—I do,' she said as he started to kiss her

shoulder, and she winced as his wandering fingers brushed her aching breasts.

His hand stilled and with the lightest touch he pulled the sheet around her, held her loosely and buried his face in her hair. Then he drew away slightly and said gently, 'I'm sorry. I must have got more carried away than I realised.' And he stroked her back.

Philippa closed her eyes and relaxed slowly. And whispered, 'It's all right—I'm all right really. At least,' she said thoughtfully, 'it helps to know you got carried away too.'

'Did you doubt it?'

She moved her shoulders in the barest little gesture that could have been a disclaimer or could have been an acknowledgement, then said, 'What will we do now? I mean, I do have to go to work today but. . .'

'What would you like to do? As a matter of fact I have to go to work too.'

'Do you mean—how will we handle things now?'

His lips twitched. 'Roughly.'

She was silent, thinking, which wasn't that easy with his hand still caressing her, then she realised that only one thing stood out in her mind—it had happened and she didn't feel like analysing it in the least.

'Do you know,' she said with a slight frown, 'what I'd like?'

'Not unless you tell me, no.'

She sat up again and said with a curious intensity, 'I'd like to take things one day at a time. No decisions, no more whys and wherefores. I'd like us to get to know each other better before we. . .' She shrugged. 'Does that make any sense? It should to *you*,' she said sternly but with a glint of something else in her eyes.

'I stand demolished,' he murmured. 'But——'

'No,' she put her finger to his lips, 'that's how I want it. I think we *both* need it. Everything that's gone before has been quite exhausting!'

'I'm inclined to agree with that,' he said wryly and drew her back into his arms. 'Are you suggesting that we should sample the peace for a change?'

'Exactly.'

'Philippa——'

'I really don't think I'd be up to anything else anyway,' she said into his shoulder. 'I mightn't be for some time. Do you always make love like that?'

'How?'

'I can't *tell* you. You must know what I mean.' A faint smile curved her lips.

'No.' He traced the outline of her mouth. 'I mean, no, I don't always. In fact I don't recall ever having made love quite like that before—all else pales into insignificance.'

Philippa raised an eyebrow. 'That's very diplomatic of you.'

'Well, how about you? If you're determined to conduct this conversation with me which. . .'

'Is in the very essence of bad taste?' she supplied. 'You're right. How did we get on to the subject?'

His eyes glinted wickedly. 'I can't think.'

She sighed, but unrepentantly. 'I was never renowned for my tact. Oh, dear, I just wish I didn't have to go to work today.'

'We still have a couple of hours up our sleeves, were we wearing any.'

Philippa smiled into his eyes and smoothed her palm across his shoulder and down his chest. 'That would be the complete undoing for me,' she whispered.

'Then,' he gathered her closer and slid his leg over hers, 'let's just rest in peace for a while.'

They did and she dozed in his arms and woke to the lovely sensation of still being in his arms, the feel of his body entwined with her, the feeling of being cherished.

'Thanks,' she said and touched his cheek.

'For what?'

'Just that. I really needed it. I might even be able to go out and slay dragons today after all. . .'

He laughed. 'That's my Philippa.'

He was also responsible for her causing a minor sensation at Colefax and Carpenter's a couple of hours later. And it had come about after they'd breakfasted and showered and she was standing at her wardrobe preparing to dress for work.

Her hand hovered and some instinct caused her to turn, to find him behind her across the room, watching her. She turned back to the wardrobe and withdrew one of her favourite dresses.

Half an hour later they parted.

At the door, he said, 'Will you have dinner with me tonight?'

'Yes—but we could have it here. I like cooking.'

He smiled at her. 'I'll bring the wine—see you then.' But he didn't touch her or attempt to kiss her and she was curiously grateful.

'My God!' Len Colefax dropped the heavy book in his hands and it hit the corner of his desk then crashed to the floor, but he appeared not to notice as he stared at Philippa. At her loose chestnut hair, her perfect skin with the barest make-up, no glasses, at her beautifully tailored, perfectly fitting pimento dress and large round gold earrings, her long legs encased in the sheerest nylon and shod in very high-heel black leather shoes.

'My God,' he said again. 'Am I seeing things? I can't believe it's you, Philippa.'

She grimaced and walked forward. 'It is indeed I, Mr Colefax,' she murmured with some irony. 'May I sit down?'

He sat down himself, still looking stunned. 'Of course.' His eyes widened. 'So it was all poppy-cock—what you told me about going to the Maldives? You went somewhere else and got yourself made over, didn't you?'

'No,' she said, and added with gentle satire, 'This is the real me. I just got tired of having to disguise myself so men would think more of my brains than. . .anything else. Which we have established—my ability—incidentally, haven't we, Mr Colefax?'

He looked at her ruefully then burst out laughing. 'Still the same old Philippa in some respects, I see. Yes, we have established that, my dear. In fact your ability has scored us a great coup, which was why I wanted to see you as soon as you got in. I still feel like pinching myself, though,' he said and shook his head amazedly. Then his eyes sharpened. 'Sure you didn't fall in love in the Maldives?'

Philippa maintained a calm expression at some cost. 'I guessed that's what you would think,' she said pleasantly, but could not quite hide the spark of contemptuous hauteur in her green eyes.

But Len Colefax grinned unashamedly and said boyishly, 'Wow—er—well, Philippa, guess what?'

'I think you'll have to tell me, I'm not much good at guessing games, Mr Colefax,' she replied tranquilly.

He sat forward, his mind wholly on business at last. 'Learmonth's have come to the party,' he said succinctly. 'Your pilot program has been such a success they want to convert all their offices to it.'

Philippa made a veal and mushroom dish for dinner with fruit salad and ice-cream for dessert and smoked salmon to begin with.

Everything was ready when Mark arrived and she still wore her pimento dress and gold earrings.

He was formally dressed too, in a lightweight cream suit and a rather imaginative bottle-green tie, and he held not only a bottle of wine but a bunch of flowers.

'Thank you,' she murmured, burying her face in the cool blossoms for a moment in a bid to hide the devastating effect his presence was having on her.

But, once inside, he took the flowers from her and drew her into his arms and proceeded to kiss her thoroughly and hungrily.

And she could only lean shakily against him afterwards then say, 'Perhaps I shouldn't have bothered with dinner—I don't know if I'm up to eating.'

He laughed softly and brushed her lips lightly with his, then stood her away from him. 'We have to eat, and whatever it is smells delicious.'

It was delicious, and they talked desultorily until Philippa said suddenly, 'You didn't tell me that Learmonth's want to convert completely.'

He sat back and watched the golden wine in his glass. 'We didn't get the chance to discuss mundane matters like that yesterday.'

She raised an eyebrow. 'It might be mundane to you, but Len Colefax is—was—over the moon. Was it a purely business decision?'

'Entirely,' he said gravely, then his eyes narrowed faintly. 'Was?'

'I. . .' Philippa paused. 'I told him I didn't want to install it.'

'Why not?'

She pulled the cheeseboard towards her and cut herself a slice of smoked Cheddar. 'I should have thought that was obvious,' she said quietly, 'but the obvious aside what I told *him* was that I didn't want to have to spend extended periods in Sydney and Melbourne. He was quite distraught.'

'Philippa, that decision *was* made in a purely business context and it was mooted before we remet in the Maldives. But if that's how you feel, it's fine with me.'

She made an ironic little face. 'Could you explain that to Len Colefax?'

He was silent for a time. Then he said, 'If you like.'

She sighed. 'No, I don't like. I'd rather you didn't even mention my name to him. But it would,' she glanced at him, 'it would be awkward, wouldn't it?'

'You mean if we kept bumping into each other in lifts, et cetera? It would certainly be distracting.' He smiled briefly. 'Philippa——'

But she interrupted, 'There is the expertise at Colefax to do it, Mark.'

'All right,' his lips twitched, 'I believe you.'

'Then why do I feel guilty?' she said more to herself than him. 'I wonder if it's got anything to do with the fact that Len Colfax was right. . .' She broke off and bit her lip.

'Right about what?'

'About women being more trouble than they're worth. He. . .he once accused me of having fallen in love with you,' she said slowly and felt herself colouring beneath his narrowed scrutiny.

'No wonder you put up such a fight,' he said softly.

'That had nothing to do with it,' she retorted, but had to add wryly, 'I can just imagine how smug he'd be if he could see us now.'

He stretched out his hand and covered hers as it lay on the table. 'Can I make a suggestion? Instead of getting too analytical or bitter and twisted about the likes of Len Colefax, should we return to the strategy we agreed on this morning?'

Philippa opened her mouth to reply tartly then she sighed and smiled faintly. 'Do you mean. . .?'

'Yes, unless you only invited me for dinner, Miss Wright?'

'No,' she said helplessly, the faint disquiet at the back of her mind disappearing beneath the way he was looking at her. 'No.'

This time he took his time undressing her and his wandering fingers and lips, as he removed each article, wreaked havoc with her composure—she wasn't sure why she'd decided to be more composed, but it was a decision doomed to dismal failure as her lace and silk underwear bit the dust, in a manner of speaking, item by pale, flesh-coloured item. Then he took his clothes off without ceremony and there were no barriers between their bodies and she too could seek and explore, even tantalise a little and hold his broad shoulders beneath her hands, run her fingers into his hair, glory in the beautiful compactness and strength of his hips—and murmur his name with desire.

Afterwards, she wasn't sleepy this time, so she showered and wrapped her Male sarong around her and she heated up the coffee that they'd neglected to have earlier, and brought it to the bed. She even caught herself in the act of whistling while she waited for it to perk.

'What's funny?' he enquired as he pulled up the pillows and took his cup.

She curled up on the bed beside him, cradling her cup in both hands. Another grin curved her lips. 'Me. I feel so well I can't wondering whether you weren't right.'

'Right about. . .frustrated spinsters?' he hazarded with a glint in his eye.

'Mmm. . .' She sipped her coffee and glanced at him wryly. 'If only they *could* see me now.'

'If they could see you now,' he fiddled with some wet strands of her hair on her neck, 'they might think I'm luckier than I deserve. It's a lovely thing to see you now.'

'Will you spend the night with me?' she asked.

'I doubt if I'm capable of doing anything else. Yes. Unfortunately I'm off to Sydney for a few days tomorrow.'

Philippa smiled at him and didn't take issue with this. Instead she said, 'Do you like your lifestyle? So much travelling?'

'I did,' he said thoughtfully. 'Now I'm wondering if one outgrows it. It can make you feel rootless.'

'Well, where do you live principally?'

'Sydney now, I guess, since my father transferred our head office down there and the family more or less moved down there.'

'More or less?'

'My mother is a staunch Queenslander so she and—others, commute a lot too. She insisted on keeping the family home up here.'

'Are you artistic in any way?'

He looked at her wryly. 'I don't paint or play an instrument, but I enjoy both music and art. How about you?'

'The same, although I do play the piano and I love to dance.' She grimaced. 'It was my only saving grace in my mother's eyes. I'm sure she could never understand what she'd done to deserve a daughter with a burning interest in maths and science.'

'If your dinner was anything to go by you do have some domestic skills,' he said idly. 'And I like your flat.'

'Thanks.'

'Well, seeing as we both like music, how would it be if I got tickets for the Royal Philharmonic next week?'

'Oh, I'd love to!' Philippa said genuinely, then she hesitated and lowered her lashes.

He tilted her chin. 'What's wrong?'

'Nothing,' she said, but it was with a curious uncertainty in her voice.

His grey eyes probed hers. 'Don't you want to be seen with me?'

'It. . .has its disadvantages. Your affairs are pretty well documented, you know.'

'And a good two thirds of it is pure speculation, Philippa,' he said steadily, his fingers still on her chin.

'Perhaps,' she conceded. 'That doesn't make it any less uncomfortable to be the object of that speculation. Besides——'

'I don't honestly think going to one concert together is going to shake the world, but if you're worried about Len Colefax finding out—does that really worry you, Philippa?' he asked with a frown.

Put like that, it seemed a trivial point of pride. 'No,' she said at last. 'Thank you, I'd love to go to a concert with you.'

The next few weeks proceeded in something of a blur for Philippa.

Len Colefax was out of town having disgruntledly taken himself on holiday, still sure in his own mind that he could talk Philippa round when the time came.

As for Philippa, she attended the concert in a pinky bronze shantung suit, with her hair piled elegantly on top of her head and pearls in her ears. They didn't go unnoticed, but she saw no one she knew and escaped any social columnists and afterwards they went back to her flat and made love slowly and lingeringly, still tuned to the lovely strands of the music they'd heard

And she made no further demur about being seen out with him at restaurants occasionally and at the races once. But they spent most of their time together at her flat. Mark stayed in a hotel when in Brisbane despite the family home, and one thing she was not prepared to do was expose herself to being seen frequently going to his room. Not, she knew, that he would have expected her to.

And, for those few weeks, their relationship was unashamedly physical. It was a sweet kind of torture to be together and not to be able to touch each other.

'Oh, God,' she said once, when they'd left a meal unfinished in a restaurant, and reached her bedroom breathless and laughing but deeply affected by each other, 'this can't go on!'

They hadn't bothered with the light but there was a path of moonlight across the room and they were standing in it. Mark had opened her black silk blouse and the lacy black bra beneath and was kissing her breasts with his arms about her waist while she was arching her throat, her hands on his shoulders.

'Want to bet?' He raised his head briefly and his grey eyes glinted in the moonlight.

'I mean. . .so. . .so. . .' But she couldn't go on and she could only grip his shoulder with greater and greater urgency and not only because of what his hands and lips were doing to her, but also because of what she wanted to say and was finding harder not to each time he made love to her—I love you, I need you. I don't think I can live without you now. . .

Afterwards, he said, when she was lying in his arms, drowsy and sated, 'You don't think we can go on wanting each other like this?'

She stirred and drew her fingers down his naked back. 'Do you?'

'I'm not a clairvoyant, but at the moment I can't think of anything that could change the way I want you.'

'Except. . .' She broke off.

'What?'

She was silent, but thinking. Except living with me, day in and day out—not this rarefied relationship, this passionate but graceful affair with us both going our own way between times, but the down-to-earth, perhaps stifling business of being man and wife.

'Philippa?'

She said, 'Well, it just surprises me, that's all. I didn't think I could ever feel this. . .' She broke off and trembled inwardly.

And she thought he sighed before he said, 'Do you want to talk about—love?'

Ever afterwards she was to brand herself as a complete coward for what she replied. 'No. Not yet——'

'Philippa——'

But again she put her fingers to his mouth. 'No. I still want to take things one day at a time. It's only been a few weeks and, if nothing else, we have all the time in the world.' And she discovered that although this was a lie it gave her a curious confidence to have spoken it—as if she could persuade herself that she was not growing more and more dependent on him.

Nor was she to know, until she got a call from him two days later to say that his father had been taken seriously ill, that she wouldn't be seeing him for several weeks. Something else she wasn't to know was that Len Colefax, who had taken a hammering in the previous year's stock market crash, had been systematically and unsuccessfully trying to restore his fortunes by gambling on race-horses.

It was, coincidentally, when she discovered this plus something else, that the rest of her world started to cave in.

CHAPTER EIGHT

'PHILIPPA ——'

'Mr Colefax,' Philippa said wearily, 'I'm not going to do it.'

'*Why*? Damn it, at least tell me why,' he said intensely, and Philippa suddenly realised that he wasn't looking well, that was he looking strained and tired and. . .haunted.

She frowned and hesitated, then said, 'You won't lose the contract without me, Mr Colefax, and at least two others here are just as capable——'

'How do you know that?' he barked at her.

'You know it as well as I do——'

'You mean that I won't lose the contract?'

'I,' she paused, gathering her wits, 'mean where does it specify it has to be me?'

'It doesn't actually specify it, but they were so happy with you. It's unspoken but implicit, Philippa. Besides,' Len Colefax's shoulders slumped suddenly, 'the two others, Spencer and West, have just given notice.'

Philippa's mouth fell open. 'What?' she whispered.

'You heard me,' he answered curtly.

'Why?'

'There's an old saying about rats deserting a

sinking ship—oh, hell,' he rubbed his fleshy face, 'you can't really blame them. What puzzles me—or does it?' he muttered, 'is why you haven't caught a whiff of what is going on.' He looked at her bitterly.

'Going on?' Philippa repeated helplessly.

'This company is in imminent danger of folding, Philippa,' he said deliberately. And he told her why.

'But. . .'

'Look, it was a gamble to begin with—you must know that, it's always a gamble to take on the likes of IBM, et cetera, and I borrowed heavily to establish it in the first place, then I had to buy Carpenter out and nothing has gone right for me since, not the bloody stock market or the horses, nothing. Except,' he drew a breath and sent her a blazing glance, 'the Learmonth contract. Philippa, believe me, you are my only hope and—oh, hell, I didn't want to do this but I *know* why you're holding out, although I find it hard to believe you'd let yourself in for it. Don't you know? I told you myself about Bannister's—I also told you you were wasting your time!'

Philippa stared at him, her face paling. 'What do you know?'

'That you and Mark Learmonth are lovers,' he said with an irony that wasn't lost on her.

'How?'

'I happened to be in a restaurant one night when you and he—er—left in a hurry. I was trying to make up my mind whether to come over and say hello.'

A burning blush travelled up Philippa's throat. 'Mr Colefax,' she said shakily, 'I. . .' She stared at him helplessly until he looked away embarrassedly. 'But,' a chaotic jumble of thoughts ran through her mind, 'what's it got to do with Bannister's?' she asked, picking the least important item—or so she thought—anything to break this awful impasse.

'What's it got to do with it? Speculation is rife that they're merging. He told you himself he was expanding, he as good as told me the same thing.'

'So? I mean I understand what a big—if he wants Bannister's to convert too but. . .' She trailed off.

'Philippa, don't you know anything?' Len Colefax said despairingly. 'Don't you know that Susan Bannister has just turned nineteen, that she's gorgeous and eminently marriageable, that it's his father's dearest wish they marry and join the houses of Learmonth and Bannister for all time?'

'Susan. . . *Susan* Bannister?' Philippa said and licked her lips.

'Yes,' he said impatiently. 'She's been the sole heir to Bannister's since her parents died, they've known each other since she was a baby, he's been her trustee—Philippa, the whole damn world and its wife knows what Mark Learmonth has been waiting for!'

'But. . .it sounds like fiction more than fact,' she said huskily, and more to still the growing urge to scream. 'Do men do things like that? Marry to please their fathers? Wait for little girls to grow up—it sounds incredible!' and she stared at Len Colefax, unaware of the appeal for reassurance in her eyes.

'My dear,' he slumped in his chair, 'men marry for a variety of reasons, and when you're as experienced and perhaps as cynical as Mark is, that could be as good a reason to marry as most, if not better—I mean, Bannister's—without having to spend a cent!' He lifted his shoulders. 'But who knows?' He spread his hands. 'She might be the one to make him fall deeply in love, although I'd say he's had it his own way for a long time now.'

Philippa closed her eyes.

He said her name tentatively, then, 'Despite our differences, I'm sorry I had to be the one to let you know how things stood, and, perhaps,' he glanced at her wearily, 'I'm doing him an injustice. Perhaps *you* will be the one he falls deeply in love with.'

'But not necessarily marry,' Philippa said starkly.

Len Colefax swore. 'What a bloody mess. Did he tell you he didn't want you to do the job?'

'No,' she whispered, 'he said it was up to me. He. . .didn't seem to mind one way or another.' Oh, God, she thought, I knew there was something wrong about that. I wanted *him* to say there'd be no question of my working on the Learmonth account. . .

A spark of compassion that actually surprised Len Colefax gripped him, but Philippa's white face and trembling lips were hard to resist. 'What will you do?' he added gently.

'I'll do it,' Philippa heard herself say as if from a great distance. 'But I'd rather do it from here——'

'Philippa—oh, hell, I don't see how you can.' He sat back and sighed defeatedly. 'I might as well give up.'

'No,' Philippa said slowly. 'I've thought of a plan. One of the supervisors in their office here impressed me very much. I think with some extra coaching from us, she could handle the training in their other offices—it's in their interests to have someone of their own with as much knowledge as possible too. What do you think?'

Two nights later Mark rang her from Sydney, catching her off guard because she was in the shower.

'Hello?' she said breathlessly into the phone.

'Philippa?'

'Oh. Yes. How are you?'

'Fine.' But he sounded clipped and curt.

'Is your father. . .?'

'Worse, I'm afraid.'

'I'm sorry,' she said quietly.

'What are you doing?'

'I was having a shower—I'm dripping all over the floor,' she said brightly.

He laughed briefly. 'Normally we're dripping together—haven't you even got a towel on?'

'I have but I'm still dripping.'

'That's a pity—I was picturing you *au naturel*—but I can make the adjustment.'

Philippa bit her lip. 'What are you doing?' she asked quietly.

'Having a meal before I go back to the hospital. Julia and I are taking it in turns. My mother won't leave his side.'

'Oh.'

'Is something wrong?'

Dreadfully wrong, she wanted to say, but how can I tell you at a time like this? 'I. . .' She stopped and bit her lip, then said in a rush, 'Would you like me to come down?'

There was a short silence at the other end then he said wearily, 'No. I think I'm best spending all the time I possibly can with him, but thank you.'

'It's all right,' she said slowly. 'Well,' she added, 'I'll be. . .thinking of you.'

'The same here,' he said quietly.

She put the phone down and blinked away sudden hot tears, and helplessly continued the battle she'd been waging with herself for the last two days. . . If his father was dying would he not at least want to introduce her to him? Or *was* it his father's dearest wish that he married Susan Bannister?

A new twist to a two-day-old conundrum, she thought drearily, that began thus: would Len Colefax stoop to incredibly cunning lengths to get her to change her mind? Yet when you'd seen the love shining out of Susan Bannister's eyes with your *own* eyes it all had a curiously authentic ring about it. And when you added the facts that Mark Learmonth could be ruthless—she shivered suddenly—that he'd had the pick of the crop for years, that he believed love was a very rare commodity, that her own father had warned her he was a tough businessman. . .

She closed her eyes and pressed her fingers to her mouth as she thought further. Then there's the fact that he didn't seem to mind one way or the other whether I went back to Learmonth's. Did he. . .did he even think it would keep me handy but ensure we would have to be very discreet?

The prospect appalled her but she couldn't quite bring herself to believe it of Mark. And it occurred to her that she had the choice of believing Len Colefax or believing in Mark. Not, she thought, that she could doubt that Len himself believed what he'd told her, on reflection. Because if he hadn't been desperate he'd probably never have mentioned it at all. Because if it wasn't true and she took it all to Mark, Len would lose the Learmonth contract, as he had to be aware. Even if it was and Mark found out who'd told her, he could still lose the contract. But had it actually gone on record, for example, as being the dearest wish of Winston Learmonth—who could be dying now? Or was it one of those rumours Mark had unwittingly fuelled over the years?

She closed her eyes and buried her head in her hands, but she couldn't banish from her mind's eye the genuine embarrassment she'd seen in her boss's eyes, and she couldn't help wondering what she'd see in her father's and her brother's eyes if it ever came out that she was Mark Learmonth's mistress.

She had several short phone calls from Mark over the next days then, on a Saturday morning, she answered her doorbell and he was standing on the doorstep.

She gasped, for several reasons, but one of them was the way he looked. Impeccably dressed in a lightweight grey suit, white shirt and blue tie but obviously exhausted and with lines of strain around his mouth she'd never seen before.

'Oh. . .' Her eyes widened. 'Has. . .?'

'No. The crisis is over and he's going to recover, but it will be a long, slow haul.'

'I'm so happy for you. . .'

'Philippa?' He reached for her and buried his face in her hair. 'I've *missed* you, but I'm out on my feet. They had to shovel me off the plane. . .'

She held him and felt her heart beating slowly and loudly and knew there was only one thing she wanted to do. Restore him.

'Come,' she said softly.

She'd made her bed up freshly that morning and she helped him take his clothes off and slide between the crisp sheets. Then she drew the curtains and lay down beside him but above the sheets, and stroked his back.

'This wasn't exactly the kind of reunion I had in

mind,' he murmured, and smiled with an effort as he slid his fingers through her hair.

'It doesn't matter. Relax.'

'That's what I don't seem to be able to do.'

'Yes, you will,' she said softly. 'Trust me.'

And beneath the slow massage of her fingers he was asleep five minutes later, but she lay with him for a long time until his first restless sleep deepened and he was breathing quietly and evenly. And as she lay watching his face lose its lines of strain and become peaceful at last, she was struck by the burden of truth—she loved this man, whatever, and it was a deeper, wider emotion than she'd ever experienced. But it was also by its very depth and breadth not possible for her to handle fragmentedly. It would, she thought with a shiver, have to be all or nothing, otherwise as it tore her apart it would kill anything they did have. Because that's me, she thought with sudden tears in her eyes.

He slept until late afternoon and she spent the day as she usually did on Saturdays, pottering about her flat, catching up on the housework and her laundry, watching a movie on television in the afternoon and then beginning to prepare dinner for them.

That was how he found her, in the kitchen with a butcher's apron over her jeans and blouse and chopping up celery for a salad.

'Well,' she said as his arms slipped round her

waist from behind and he kissed her neck, 'feeling better?' And went on chopping celery.

'Yes—I'm not disturbing you, am I?'

'Not at all,' she replied demurely and reached for a tomato, but his hand slid down her arm and removed the knife from her fingers. Then he gathered both her hands to her waist and she leant back against him.

Which helped because, by the time he turned her to face him, she had her eyes under control.

He wore only a towel hitched around his hips and, although his skin was still warm from the bed, his eyes were clear and grey and the lines of strain hadn't returned.

'I am feeling better,' he said softly. 'But there is one thing that will complete the cure.' He moved his hands lingeringly across her shoulders.

'You're starving—a good meal?' she suggested. 'I have two fillet steaks, chips and a salad.'

He observed her gravely with his head to one side and his hair falling in his eyes so that he had to squint slightly but it didn't hide the glint in them as he said, 'You're going to make me wait, aren't you?'

'I'm going to make you wait,' she agreed equally gravely. 'One should never rush a cure and you'll feel even better and stronger once you've eaten—besides which, eating can be a sensuous pleasure too. Did you know that?'

'I know that there have been times——' he brought his arms up around her neck and rested his chin on her hair '—when it's been impossible to eat.'

She kissed his throat. 'This time will be different. Why don't you have a shower or a long soak in the bath—I'll bring you a drink—and let me get the steaks on the grill?'

'Yes, Miss Wright,' he murmured, but he kissed her thoroughly before he let her go.

'Philippa?'

They'd eaten their steaks leisurely and pleasurably and played some music while they'd had coffee and talked desultorily, and it had been warm and peaceful.

Now, as he said her name and she looked across at him, it was suddenly different. Why? she wondered. Why am I feeling nervous and unsure of myself? Because I am unsure of myself, obviously, but it's different again. . . I feel like a girl with her first lover.

'Yes?'

His grey eyes scanned her face, her hair that was tied back with a ribbon tonight, the pulse at the base of her throat where her shirt opened that was suddenly doing a rapid tattoo.

'Is something wrong?'

'Yes. . .'

She was sitting on the settee, he was lounging back in a chair opposite, but he got up and came over to her. She hesitated and stared up at him. He'd changed into his blue cotton trousers and a white T-shirt after his soak in the bath, and he'd washed his hair and dried it perfunctorily and not bothered to brush it—yet none of these comforting signs of the intimacy between them comforted her at all, she found as she lowered her gaze and made room for him.

'Tell me,' he said quietly as he sat down beside her but didn't attempt to take her in his arms.

'You. . .make me nervous,' she said slowly and smiled faintly, but it wasn't an amused smile.

He raised an eyebrow. 'Why?'

'I don't know—I feel. . .' She shrugged.

'This has come up out of the blue.'

She laid her head back. 'If you must know, I feel about seventeen and as if I've never made love before. Silly, isn't it?'

He said nothing for a time, then, 'I can't take exception to that.' And stretched his arm along the back of the settee to stroke her cheek lightly with his fingers.

'But it's ridiculous! Why?'

'Perhaps it has something to do with the fact that we haven't seen each other for a fortnight. But,' he paused, 'most of the time you're more mature than most, so—is it a problem?'

'Am I?'

His fingers kept stroking. 'Yes. I don't often feel there's an eleven-year age-gap between us.'

'Is there. . .does an age-gap matter between a man and a woman?'

'No—not in someone you find desirable. In fact immaturity, dependence and vulnerability can be powerful attractions in themselves to men.'

Philippa bit her lip. 'I don't see why being more mature most of the time should make me feel like this.'

'Do you resent it?'

She thought, but could only come up with, 'If I can't help it, why resent it, but yes, I do.' 'Although it will probably only ever be a temporary aberration with me, this feeling.' And she turned her head so she could look into his eyes with something like a challenge in her own.

He looked amused. 'I didn't say *I* was one of those men, necessarily.'

But you didn't take exception. . . The thought ran through her mind, then, What am I trying to do? Evoke and at the same time erase the ghost of Susan Bannister, who is sixteen years younger than he is, who is fresh and pliable and would never dream of saying no to him? Am I trying to let him know that, while I can be a battleaxe, I still tremble and go hot and cold sometimes just to think of him making love to me, like now?

She moved restlessly then stood up abruptly. 'I guess the cure is complete—let's go to bed.'

He stared up at her narrowly then he got up himself without saying anything and took her hand.

She turned towards the bedroom door but he pulled her back and into his arms. 'No, Philippa. Not until you tell me what's really on your mind.'

'I. . .' She tried to free herself but it was useless, and her ribbon came undone and her hair adrift and her green eyes glittered with sudden anger and she said before she could stop herself, 'If you don't *know*, it would be useless trying to tell you. I. . .' She stopped and her eyes widened incredulously as she realised she was doing it already, tearing any hope she might have of this man loving her to shreds. And all because of what Len Colefax had told her and without any real corroboration. . . What would be the use of his loving me, anyway? she thought with sudden tears in her eyes. I'd probably always find reasons to doubt it. . . Is that the kind of person I really am?

'Philippa,' he said harshly, and his lean fingers dug into the soft flesh of her upper arms.

She winced, but the little shock of it helped them both perhaps. He let her go with a sudden sigh and she gathered some of her wits.

'I'm doing it again, aren't I?' she said shakily. 'Working myself into a frenzy over nothing. I don't suppose *that* will only ever be a temporary aberration with me, but if it's any. . .excuse this time, I missed you, too,' she said huskily.

His eyes were sombre and compassionate, 'My dear,' he started to say but Philippa stopped him.

'No,' she said very quietly. 'I don't think this is the time to have that discussion. You can't be thinking too straight after having come so close to losing your father. And I don't think we've given ourselves enough time yet, anyway. . .have we?'

His grey gaze didn't waver. 'If you believe that then I'll say no more. But I could tell you about some of the complications of my life which have suddenly become realities, whereas before they were. . .' He shrugged. 'On the other hand, if this state of affairs is hurting you, perhaps it's better for me to go until——'

'Go?' she said softly. 'Do you imagine that won't hurt me?'

'No. But——'

'Could you tell me just one thing?' she broke in.

'I can tell you everything——'

'No,' she whispered. 'Just one. Have you ever felt so strongly attracted to anyone before?'

His grey eyes were narrowed and intent, as if he was trying to see into her heart. And there were a few moments' silence before he said deliberately, 'No. Never. Otherwise I'd have been able to walk away from you instead of—what did happen.'

'Are you trying to say you sensed what kind of trouble I'd be for you?'

'Philippa—yes.' A nerve flicked in his jaw. 'Also the kind of trouble I might be for you. But aren't we being premature? I thought we'd decided. . .you were quite adamant you didn't want to be rushed into anything.'

For my sins, she thought, yes, I was quite adamant. Was that passionate monologue a subtle defence mechanism, a typically Philippa Wright bid to assert my independence, a point of pride to be able to claim a prerogative as much as he might? Or was it simply because I knew I was doomed to love Mark Learmonth. . .? Doomed, she thought with an inward shiver. Was I right? Haven't I just had my corroboration?

'Yes. I did, I still am,' she said quietly.

'Then shouldn't we keep the bedroom a combat-free zone—as we also decided?'

'A. . .?' Her shoulders sagged but her lips twitched suddenly and she made a strangely husky little sound in her throat when he cupped her cheek, and she turned her mouth into his palm in a gesture of acquiescence.

Their lovemaking had a new dimension. It was slower, gentler, unbearably sweet, she thought once, as they lay in each other's arms, touching, relaxed, savouring their knowledge of each other, giving taking, talking. . .

'I always suspected there might be a revelation beneath those clothes you wore.' He plucked one nipple idly then the other.

'Did you? Because of my wrists and ankles?'

His hand left her breasts and he picked up her wrist, circling it in his long fingers. 'Not only that—they looked curiously young and defenceless—but the way you moved, even in flat shoes.'

'I suppose,' she said as he placed her hand over his heart, 'it was your hands that really got me in.'

He raised an eyebrow.

She smiled and picked up his hand and placed it over her heart. 'Didn't you know women are great connoisseurs of men's hands? And their eyes.'

'What about the rest of it?'

She shrugged delicately. 'Skinny shoulders and a pot-belly don't help of course but I'm not sure that bulging biceps do so much, either. Not for me, anyway.'

He grinned lazily. 'Bulging biceps.'

'Yes,' she agreed solemnly. 'I was quite sure you'd have them.'

He grimaced. 'You obviously associate them with that old saying—all brawn and no brain. That's not altogether fair.'

'No,' she agreed. 'Especially since I knew you had a brain.'

His lips twitched. 'But you're not in the least repentant? No, well, that's my Philippa. For my part, I thought—I wonder what she's like with that make-up scraped off? Without her clothes? Her skin, where you can see it,' he slid his hands round her neck, 'looks good, so perhaps there are pearly luscious breasts beneath the camouflage; pale, voluptuous thighs.' His hand moved down her body slowly but his eyes never left hers and, although they were very grey and grave, she was not deceived for a moment.

She said severely, 'I always knew men couldn't help mentally undressing women.'

'I guess that's the way things are between men and women,' he agreed. 'But the facts,' he slid his hand back up and around the curve of her hips to her waist, the slight curve of her stomach and the triangle of curls below, 'exceeded my expectations by miles.'

'I haven't really got that overblown kind of hourglass figure, have I?' she said softly, touching now in return.

He laughed quietly. 'No. Your body is perfect, Philippa. Slender in the right places, full in the right places—don't you know?'

'I know,' she said with an effort because of what he was doing to her, 'that aerodynamically, for example, it's not supposed to be suited to swimming.'

'Ah—that rings a bell.' He propped himself up on one elbow and observed the slight flush that had come to her cheeks. Then he said consideringly, 'Is that so much worse than drawing sweeping conclusions about bulging biceps?'

'Oh, God.' But she was laughing and she buried her face in his chest and he held her closer, and they laughed together and it was warm and funny and tender, until his hands moved on her again and the inevitable fever began to beat and pulse through their bodies and their union and their release was a mutual act that closed out the rest of the world, and the doubts.

'Of course,' she said apropos of nothing the next morning, as she made breakfast and he sat at the kitchen table reading the Sunday paper, 'we couldn't spend all of our life in bed.'

He glinted an amused grey glance her way. 'Are you asking me or telling me?'

'Neither. I'm theorising,' she replied tranquilly.

'Go on, then.'

She raised her eyes heavenwards and placed a pancake in front of him with a choice of lemon juice and sugar or butter and honey. 'Help yourself,' she said a little tartly. 'I mean—we're better there than out of it, aren't we?'

He looked at her seriously. 'I've the feeling I ought to think carefully before I answer that one, but as to your original theorem, perhaps we could work out a ratio whereby the amount of time we spent in bed enveloped the rest of our time with its aura, *thereby* taking care of our naturally aggressive, combative instincts—at other times. You're the one who's good at algorithms,' he added idly.

Philippa was staring at him with her mouth open, her pancake on a plate held aloft in her hand, and he smiled lazily at her expression.

He said softly, 'I also think I'd better take you back to bed before I collect a plate and a pancake round the earhole.'

'Of all the *cold*-blooded——' she started to say but he was on his feet in one lithe movement and he wrested the plate from her, captured her wrists and said,

'*Cold*? I don't think that's ever going to be a problem for us, Philippa.' He bent his head to kiss her thoroughly.

She stood in his arms afterwards, breathing erratically, resting against him. 'No, perhaps you're right,' she whispered. 'When do you have to go?'

He kissed the top of her head, but gently. 'This afternoon—I'm sorry things have to be this way at the moment but it was impossible to keep the news about my father away from the Press, which has caused the inevitable speculation about the future of Learmonth's. Which means I'll be as busy as hell for a while.'

'Will you. . .?' Philippa stopped.

'Will I?'

'No, it doesn't matter,' she said barely audibly, then, 'Would you like to have your pancake before we go back to bed or a fresh one later?'

It was only when the front door of her flat closed on him that afternoon that she allowed herself to put into words what she'd started to say. 'Will you also be deciding between me and Susan Bannister?'

She stared at the door and remembered the perfection of their lovemaking, then asked herself a question—what are you playing at, Philippa? Are you playing for time, hoping against hope that the longer you can appear to remain in ignorance, the more you can bind him to you. . .?

CHAPTER NINE

THERESA WALSH from Learmonth's Brisbane office couldn't believe her good fortune and told Philippa so—several times—once, that was, she'd got over her amazement at Philippa's metamorphosis.

But it was soon evident that she had been a wise choice and she confirmed that the hierarchy at Learmonth's had jumped at the idea of having their own expert.

Philippa knew this, although not the 'jumped at' bit. She'd told Mark about the new plan and he'd studied her narrowly for a moment then agreed it could be done that way. They'd not discussed it since, but then she'd seen less and less of him lately, anyway, due to pressure of work as he'd predicted and as Theresa confirmed in her friendly way—as if Philippa was a member of the Learmonth family of employees and therefore vitally interested. Which I am, God help me, Philippa thought.

Then one day Theresa produced a real titbit and something Philippa had not known although something she was sure, Theresa said, was not a state secret because everybody was talking about it—it appeared the merger with Bannister's was to go ahead at last.

That same night, as it so often happened, when something cropped up, it cropped up again, Philippa caught a glimpse of Susan Bannister and, at the same time, realised that speculation about the merger *was* public property. It was an item on the main evening television news, an item that combined two newsworthy events—a charity film première and the cream of Sydney society arriving at it, among whom were the Waterfords with Julia looking exceedingly glamorous and Gary barely recognisable in an evening suit, Mark, and, unmistakably one of the party, Susan Bannister, merchant banking heiress. And, because they were associated with the other bit of news, the cameras remained on them longer.

Philippa sat up and stared as she subconsciously absorbed what the commentator was saying. '. . . Neither Learmonth nor Bannister executives have so far been prepared to comment on rumours that a merger between these two companies is imminent, but it is known that Susan Bannister, since the death of her parents, has been like one of the Learmonth family.'

The picture faded but two things were indelibly printed on Philippa's brain: Susan Bannister gazing up at Mark, and Julia watching Mark and Susan, happily and indulgently.

'Julia!' Philippa whispered. 'It wasn't Rory, it was *Mark* she was worried about falling under my spell. Because of Susan Bannister. . .'

The words seemed to echo around the room and suddenly, in her heart, Philippa was sure that

Mark had been thinking of marrying this girl; it had been what he'd started to say to her when she'd recommended marriage to him, it would probably have been what he would have done—until she'd crossed his bows and caught him off guard. Might still do, she thought, and wondered tormentedly if anyone could blame him. Better to take a calculated risk than to plunge into marriage with someone like me, a mass of complexes and heaven knows what. But he doesn't *love* her, she thought. Does he think it will come? Or will he be like my father? He did say once that marriage was no guarantee against anything.

Eventually she got up and turned the television off and sat in the dark thinking thoughts filled with pain, and wondering if this was how all mistresses felt, as well. Lonely, excluded. . .

She was pale, nervy and heavy-eyed the next morning which Theresa Walsh, still in her enthusiasm, did not notice, but Len Colefax did and he called her into his office.

'Sit down, Philippa. You don't look well,' he said abruptly. 'Did you happen to be watching the news on Channel Two last night by any chance?'

Philippa's eyes widened then an angry glint lit them. 'Mr Colefax——'

'I see you did. I also see,' he continued imperturbably, 'that it didn't affect you very well. Is it still on? You and Mark,' he added so that she couldn't mistake his meaning.

'Mr Colefax, I don't propose to have any further

discussions with you on the subject,' Philippa said, controlling her voice with difficulty.

He smiled drily. 'I don't blame you for feeling like that. Nor do I feel too happy with myself, believe me. I should never have said what I did in the first place——'

'Your breaking of your brotherhood of silence is quite safe with me, Mr Colefax,' she said contemptuously.

'Philippa, will you shut up and listen?' he said roughly. 'I should never have said anything because there's no way I—or anyone else—can *know* what really goes on between a man and a woman.'

'Or a man and two women?' The bitter words were out before she could help herself.

He sat back with a sigh. 'Has he told you anything about Susan Bannister?'

Philippa bit her lip.

'You might as well tell me, Philippa,' he said quietly. 'We're in this *together* whether we like it or not, since I opened my big mouth in the first place and since circumstance——' he shrugged '—has conspired against us. Has he?'

Philippa rubbed her mouth. 'No. But that's partly my fault. He has mentioned the complications that have arisen in his life.'

Len snorted, then his natural tendencies reasserted themselves. 'You can't blame him if the girl has fallen in love with him—I mean what would you have him do? Lock himself away in a monastery?'

Philippa stared at him and couldn't believe she was having this conversation with him. She rose and said coolly, 'You don't have to worry about me, Mr Colefax. A lot of this is my own fault. I laid down certain conditions, I brought much of it on myself.' But why did I bring this wall of silence on myself? she paused to wonder dully. He did offer to tell me everything and I have deceived him in a way—perhaps I've brought it on myself because I'm petrified to hear him *say* something like, I love you and want you but I'll never be able to marry you. . . I'm committed to another woman, a girl who loves me, who can also bring me not only a merchant bank but my father's dearest wish, a girl who might not bring me the passion you can but a much better balanced marriage. . . What would happen to me if he did say that? Would I be able to cope or would I. . .just disintegrate? Is that why I don't want to know, like an ostrich. . .? And does he know it—is he using it?

'Philippa. . .' She came back from her thoughts with a start as Len Colefax stood up. 'All right. I won't say any more, except this. The Harvard Business School is holding a three-week seminar on computer software and all the latest technology. With travelling time you could stretch that three weeks to a month or more if you wanted to take a short holiday. If you need an *out*,' he said significantly, 'I'll pay the expenses—apart from the holiday bit—provided you agree to give Colefax and Carpenter the benefit by accepting a six-month contract with us.'

Philippa shut her mouth with a click. 'When?'

'It starts in a week.'

'I'd never get in——'

'I'm already in—you could take my place. I was going to cancel but,' he shrugged, 'one of us ought to take advantage of it and you might even be the better one.'

'What. . .?' She cleared her throat. 'What about the Learmonth contract?'

'You were right about this Walsh woman, I've been watching her. I'll take it over myself—between us we could cope, I reckon.'

'Can. . .can I think about it?'

He eyed her a shade cynically. 'Sure. But you haven't got much time. You'll need a visa.'

CHAPTER TEN

Two months later, to the day, Philippa wearily unlocked her front door, pushed her two large bags through, wasn't distracted by the telephone and didn't leave her keys in the door.

It was a cool May evening but she'd been much colder during the past weeks, spiritually as well as physically.

She looked around but her flat was exactly as she'd left it.

There was a small pile of mail on her dining-room table—mail that had arrived too late to be forwarded—but none of it looked worth the bother of opening and nothing, apparently, from Mark.

Did I expect anything? she asked herself. And winced at the knowledge that a seed of hope had lurked in her heart. The hope that he would look beyond the bare words of her letter to him, posted the day she left for the States—'I've decided to end our affair. I think it's best for us both. I don't think I'm cut out to be your wife, or anyone's, perhaps. Goodbye. . .'

She stared unseeingly across the room, then she deliberately poured herself a drink which she took to the bathroom and sipped while she tried to soak away some of her jet lag so she could try to sleep.

Two mornings later she went back to work, although she wasn't expected until the next day.

She chose a long-sleeved navy blue and white patterned silk dress with a navy rough linen blazer to wear and, to strike a firm, bright note, picked a scarlet geranium from her window-box and stuck it into her lapel. She'd lost every trace of her Maldivian and Queensland summer tan, but her skin was good enough to bear being pale and her hair was glossy and rich—it had thrived although she had lost weight.

Sandra, who doubled as receptionist and Len Colefax's secretary, was surprised to see her a day early but apparently pleased. 'Mr Colefax will be delighted,' she confided. 'Things are humming here!'

'Good.' Philippa smiled at her. 'Then I'll go in and see him straight away.' And she turned away without noticing the girl's sudden frown, but the phone rang and someone else walked in.

Philippa knocked, received an irritated invitation to enter and did so. And stopped on the threshold as if she'd walked into a sheet of glass. Because Mark Learmonth was with Len Colefax.

For a long time afterwards, she was to remember the little frozen tableau they made—she with her hand still on the doorknob; Len, his mouth dropping open, behind his desk; Mark, straightening from something he'd been studying on the desk and turning his head.

It was he who broke it. 'Well, Miss Wright has returned to our midst,' he murmured, turning fully and pushing his hands into the pockets of his well-cut fawn trousers as he leant back against the desk and observed her with all the considerable detachment of which he was capable. He wore a cream shirt beneath the fawn suit with a dark red tie, and nothing had changed about him at all.

Philippa blinked then swallowed and felt the heat rise from the base of her throat in a flush she couldn't control, a searing, damning, dead giveaway.

Len Colefax stood up and said exasperatedly, 'Philippa! You're not due until tomorrow.'

Mark raised a sardonic eyebrow. 'Nothing's going to change by tomorrow, Len. Why don't you tell her the good news now?'

Len snorted. 'I've got a better idea. Why don't *you* tell her? I'll leave you two alone for a moment.' He walked towards the door, hesitated as he came abreast of Philippa with something embarrassed and at the same time helpless in his eyes, then went out, prising the doorknob from her fingers and giving her a little push into the room.

Philippa gripped her hands together, swallowed again and said, 'What are you doing here?'

He smiled but it didn't reach his eyes nor did he move, and it was a stunning insult to her—that he should look so completely at home lounging against Len's desk while she was both hot and cold and still standing stranded in the middle of the room.

'Is that how ex-lovers greet each other?' he said musingly. 'I suppose there's not much else to say. I'm only surprised you haven't resumed your battleaxe disguise. As a matter of interest,' his eyes lingered on the hollow at the base of her throat where a pulse was beating erratically then moved down to her smart outfit but as if it weren't there and that grey gaze somehow contrived to make her feel cold and naked, before returning to her stunned green eyes, 'did you not think I might merit some kind of a proper explanation?'

'*You* might. . .' The words were torn from her but she clamped her lips shut then and had to turn away blindly towards the door.

'Don't go, Philippa,' he said mildly. 'There are other things we have to discuss. Such as how you're going to enjoy working for me for the next six months.'

'What. . .?' It came out as a hoarse whisper and she swung back in spite of herself, her eyes dark and shocked.

He said amusedly, 'I thought that might stop you in your tracks. My dear, I think you'd better sit down because the reason I'm here is this. I've bought the controlling interest in Colefax and Carpenter and, thus, have also bought your contract.'

Philippa did sit down, or rather she groped towards a chair and sank into it because her legs felt incapable of supporting her.

He watched her enigmatically. 'That comes as quite a shock, obviously,' he murmured.

'Obviously,' she repeated and licked her lips. 'But why?'

He moved his shoulders in a gentle shrug. 'Two reasons: Len was in a spot of bother, and, now that Learmonth's and Bannister's have amalgamated, I really need your expertise, Philippa. Especially as *updated* as it is now.'

Their gazes locked and all the natural colour drained from Philippa's face as she whispered, 'Did you marry. . .her?'

'Would it matter one whit to you that I have—I presume we're talking about Susan?' he said ironically. 'Or is that why you ran away again?'

'You didn't *tell* me about her, but——' She stopped and stared at him, going from pale to ashen as his words sank in.

'*You* didn't want to know, not from me, that is,' he said coldly.

'All the same, I did come to know,' she said shakily. 'And I knew you well enough to know—tell me this, did it honestly never cross your mind to. . .wait for Susan Bannister to grow up? And can you deny that she's in love with you or that it was your father's dearest wish?'

'Oh, no,' he said softly but with menace, 'I can't deny any of those things——'

'Then can you deny this? That is *suited* you to prolong the way I wanted things to be, that it even occurred to you that you could have us both—Susan with a ring on her finger and me on the side. What a happy arrangement, especially while I was working on the Learmonth contract and then, no doubt, Bannister's!'

If she'd ever made Mark Learmonth angry before, it was nothing compared to this, she could tell from the white shade about his mouth, the murderous glint in his grey eyes, the sudden abrupt way he pulled his hands from his pockets. Then it was all gone as swiftly as it had come and the indifference that was like a blow was back.

As he drawled, 'Then there's one thing you neglected to *tell* me, isn't there, Philippa? How desperate you were to marry me yourself. Well, perhaps we've learned enough home truths this session. Until next time, Miss Wright.' And he strolled out.

'Oh, my God,' Len Colefax said desperately as he returned to take possession of his office—to find Philippa still sitting there, weeping distractedly into her hands.

'What am I going to do?' She raised her tear-streaked face. 'How *could* you sell my contract to him?'

'He wouldn't buy me out without it,' Len said urgently. 'God knows—if *you* only knew how I'm beginning to regret I ever so much as mentioned the name of Learmonth to you, Philippa, ever!'

She stood up convulsively. 'If only *you* knew how bitterly I regret ever having heard the name of Colefax and Carpenter, let alone ever having darkened your doors—but I'll be taking legal action over this, Mr Colefax. So don't expect to see me until I've consulted my lawyer.' She swept out.

She couldn't sleep that night—she hadn't been able to eat or do anything but pace her flat all day in the grip of a despair such as she'd never known. But why? she'd kept asking herself anguishedly. He has married her—he would have done it even if I hadn't run away. He's no better than any of them—in fact he's worse. Oh! How can you hate someone and still feel so. . .bereft?

'This is quite a tangle,' the Wright family lawyer said to her the next morning. 'You appear to have signed a watertight contract, Philippa.'

'But I signed it with Colefax and Carpenter—surely the fact that Learmonth's have bought into the company changes things.'

'But it's still ostensibly Colefax and Carpenter——'

'When I signed that,' Philippa said with barely controlled patience, 'it was on the understanding that I knew who I would be working for—that was *why* I signed it. *If* I'd known I would be working for. . .well, someone else, I might not have signed it, so I must have some right of. . of. . .' She broke off and stared at the lawyer frustratedly.

'That's true,' he said slowly 'However, and *whoever*, the other party has fulfilled their side of the contract. You've received a partly expenses-paid trip to America plus a seminar, et cetera, and you can't hand that back now, *per se* Although you could return the costs—Philippa, leave it with me for a few days. This is not quite up my street but I can take advice on it.'

And with that she had to be content.

But that afternoon she received an urgent telephone call from Len Colefax's secretary to the effect that Len had been taken to hospital with chest pains and that his last words to her had been to contact Philippa and beg her to come in and hold the fort for a couple of days at least.

Which, reluctantly, she did.

There was no sign of Mark Learmonth and she resolutely ignored any business concerning the Learmonth take-over of Colefax and Carpenter, and concentrated on the programs in hand. And for a week she worked on what was after all her forte, and was unwittingly soothed by it. Soothed enough to even think that she was cut out above all to be a career women *after* all. Just. . .leave love alone, she mused once. It obviously doesn't work for you. She even managed to banish the insidious images of Mark and Susan Bannister-Learmonth, who probably thought all her Christmases had come at once, who would love him unstintingly and therefore be vulnerable and defenceless enough, as well as young enough, not to be hurt, to be treated with care, to be cherished and never to know, if she was lucky, the other side of him, the basic cruel indifference. Either that or end up like my mother, she thought cynically.

Len Colefax in the meantime was discharged

from hospital, his chest pains a matter of some mystery to his physicians, who nevertheless, to be on the safe side, cautioned him to take things very quietly for a time.

It crossed Philippa's mind that this had been a stylish, diplomatic indisposition, then she immediately felt a touch of guilt and also thought, wearily, I'm better back at work so long as I can keep out of Mark's way. I'd be a raving lunatic sitting at home and twiddling my thumbs and waiting to find out if I have any hope of fighting this contract. And I don't suppose he'll be exactly haunting the office now. . .

But although a week could be a long time in politics, it was not, she discovered the next day, nearly long enough to heal a broken heart.

They arrived together at the entrance to the building that housed the offices of Colefax and Carpenter on the tenth floor—Philippa from one direction and striding out through the crisp, chilly but clear morning because, although she was early, she was also in a fury of impatience to reach the haven of work where she could submerge herself, Mark from a chauffeur-driven Mercedes, and they all but bumped into each other on the pavement.

'Oh,' she breathed with a swift upward glance as she swerved at the last moment, then there was a momentary freezing of all her faculties.

'Philippa,' he said drily. 'On your way to work? Or to a fire?'

Her faculties unfroze but she bit her lip on any

retort and marched up the steps. He followed and so did a thin stream of other early birds so that there was a group of about ten people waiting at the bank of lifts. Two lifts arrived at the same time and the group divided itself into roughly equal proportions, so although she would have preferred eight strangers, she still had three to share the lift with her and Mark Learmonth.

But the three people all got out at lower and different floors, so it was a slow progression to the tenth. During which time he leant his shoulders casually against the lift wall and steadily surveyed her profile.

The chill, fresh morning had brought colour to her cheeks and a sparkle to her appearance and her green fine wool coat matched her eyes and brought out the chestnut glints in her hair. But it was all an illusion—at least, there was nothing sparkling about the way her heart was beating heavily and like a muffled drum.

She refused to look at him but could feel his steady scrutiny through her pores and, by the time they did reach the tenth floor, the colour in her cheeks was not only because of her brisk walk through the morning air.

Sandra must have arrived just ahead of them because she was taking off her coat as Mark held the door open for Philippa, and she greeted them cheerfully.

'Morning, Mr Learmonth, Philippa. Would you like a cup of coffee, Mr Learmonth?' she added obligingly. 'I always get Mr Colefax one first thing.'

'Thank you, Sandra, but could you make it two? Miss Wright and I have some things to discuss. We'll be in Mr Colefax's office.'

Philippa opened her mouth, hesitated because he was making it patently obvious she should lead the way and Sandra was still disposing of her handbag and coat, then she turned towards Len Colefax's office.

He closed the door behing them and said quietly, 'Would *you* like to take your coat off before you sit down, Philippa?'

'I. . .but we don't have anything to discuss so. . .'

'No? Not even how the office is to survive without Len for the next fortnight?'

'It's survived before,' Philippa said cynically.

'That's isn't how we do things at Learmonth's,' he observed. 'Nor do we believe that when the weight can be carried by someone else, and often is, it should go unrewarded. So that's something else we have to discuss, Philippa. Whether you would accept a junior partnership.'

Five minutes later, Philippa was still in a state of shock and, in the interim, she had handed him her coat—although she didn't remember it—she'd smoothed down her matching green linen dress, the coffee had arrived and she was sitting across Len's desk from Mark Learmonth with her cup steaming gently in front of her.

'Does Mr Colefax know about this?' Her voice

was uncertain and husky and her uncertainty was mirrored in her eyes.

Mark watched her for a moment and she trembled inwardly as so many memories lit her mind one after the other. . .

'Yes. And he approves. You're his key personnel member now. Without you Colefax and Carpenter doesn't have much to offer; your expertise has outstripped his, although his business experience is much greater. You two,' he paused, studied the desk then lifted his grey eyes, 'also understand each other rather well. We feel, at Learmonth's, that it will be a good working combination.'

For just one brief moment, Philippa discovered she felt like dying as she wondered how what she had shared with Mark Learmonth could have come to this, and whether this was her pay-off. For services rendered? Or for having had the temerity to turn her back on him. Did he know how dearly it would cost her to have to go on working for him, with him sometimes, did he know and had even calculated the pain. . .?

'Why are you doing this?' she whispered involuntarily. 'Please, at least be honest with me.'

Their gazes clashed but it was with his same indifference that he said, 'I don't think we've dealt much in honesty, you and I, Philippa, but you did once say you didn't believe you were cut out to be anyone's wife and, more particularly, not mine, so here is an opportunity to really be the other thing, a career woman.'

'And you——' her voice shook but she made herself go on '—immediately went out and *took* a wife, so no, perhaps we haven't dealt much in honesty.'

'Philippa, I——'

She cut him off contemptuously. 'But then I always knew it was on the cards you would marry Susan Bannister.' She was having trouble keeping her hands still, her lips from trembling, so she made herself drink some coffee and made herself concentrate on its reviving effects. 'One thing,' she said eventually. 'If I accept this you must understand there can be no going back——'

'You mean I can't have you on the side—your choice of words, I believe,' he murmured and stared at her with brutal mockery. 'Let's not beat about the bush, Philippa. Why not? It would only be what we both want.'

She stared back, unable to articulate and with a faint roaring sound in her ears.

He watched her dispassionately for a moment then said smoothly, 'Besides, can you do without it now? You told me once you were in a bad way without me. I'd say,' his eyes slid thoughtfully down her figure, examined her wrists in her lap, 'you've lost a fair bit of weight, my dear, and I should imagine it won't be long before you're back to terrorising any man you can lay your hands on even without your disguise. Look, let's be reasonable, Susan need never know, you can keep your precious career—it would be a perfect working arrangement.'

I'm not hearing this—this is not real, the dazed thought stumbled through her mind. 'No,' she breathed. 'I——'

'Why don't you at least give it some thought?' he drawled. 'I can assure you you wouldn't——' he paused '—come out of it empty-handed. I'd take over the payments for your flat while it continued. I certainly wouldn't expect you to behave like a conventional mistress, and by that I mean you wouldn't have to sit at home waiting for me every night, although, on the other hand, I won't have any trouble getting away frequently. You don't have a car, do you? We could remedy that and it would be no trouble at all to—engineer an overseas holiday once a year. We could even try the Maldives again, seeing as our last trip there was rather an abortive affair.' He raised an eyebrow and waited.

'You. . .you are even worse than I suspected you might be—you're the most incredible sham, Mark Learmonth. Oh. . .' She dropped her face into her hands.

'Am I?' he said meditatively and with an odd tinge of irony, but when she looked up at last he went on almost immediately, 'I take it you're saying no? All right. Then let's take the purely businesslike approach. Let me tell you how a partnership, even a junior one, will benefit you. These are the terms we had in mind.' And he outlined them briefly and precisely—terms that in other circumstances would have been like all *her* Christmases come at once. And he finished by saying, 'But you don't have to decide immediately, Philippa. Think it over, although there's still your old contract.' He shrugged. 'It might be a little expensive for you to get out of it but naturally, if you accepted this offer, we wouldn't expect you to finish it before these terms came into effect.'

Philippa swallowed several times to prevent herself from doing several things: bursting into tears, doing something essentially violent like throwing the rest of her coffee over him, *telling* him that she must have been mad to imagine she loved him, mad to have agonised over him and lost weight for him. . .

She stood up and said crisply, 'I don't need to think it over, thank you. I accept. And, despite what you might like to think, this will be a perfect and *purely* business arrangement. You will have to look elsewhere for your extramarital diversions, Mark Learmonth, but, if I were you, I wouldn't parade them too closely in front of me. Because they not only wouldn't affect me in the slightest but they might just prompt me to enlighten your poor wife—who knows what a battleaxe like myself would do in the heat of the moment?'

He laughed softly and stared up into her coldly furious green eyes. 'Do your damnedest, Philippa. I always knew hell had no fury like a woman scorned.'

He might even be partly right, she thought, as she worked feverishly through the morning, about hell having no fury like mine, but if he knew whose scorn was the greater. . . How did I ever. . .? But no, it's *over*, and I have the opportunity not only to prove to him how very over it all is, but also to enrich myself and advance my career in great leaps. We'll see who'll have the last laugh.

Her fury carried her through to late afternoon, when Len Colefax put in an appearance. Mark had apparently left the office mid-morning for Sydney.

'Well, Mr Colefax,' she said with brittle brightness as she responded to his summons, 'how are you—and should you be here at all?'

Len grimaced. 'I'll be fine so long as I take things easy for a while. Did you. . .have you. . .?' He cocked a wary eyebrow at her.

Philippa glanced round his office and decided she hated the place. 'I did and I have—I do hope it *was* with your approval that the offer was made?'

'Oh, it was,' he assured her. 'I just wasn't quite sure how you would react.'

She smiled thinly and said deliberately, 'Certain things, which I propose never to discuss with you again, have finally been resolved. In the negative. Although,' she glanced at him bitterly, 'now he has a wife I don't see how you could have expected anything different. Or are all men really alike?' she added caustically.

Len Colefax shut his mouth with a click then said nervously, 'Who has a wife?'

She looked at him wearily. 'Mark Learmonth—who else?'

'Philippa, he doesn't,' Len said hoarsely. 'Who did you think he'd married?'

She stared at him and whispered, 'Susan Bannister, of course. . .'

'No—oh, I see—because of the merger! But no, it didn't need that, and she's gone to Paris to study art and languages at the Sorbonne. . . *Philippa*, where have you *been*?'

'In America, in my own pain-filled little world—oh, *why* didn't you tell me?'

'I didn't get much opportunity, but I never thought you'd just jump to that conclusion,' he said helplessly.

'*Jump* to it—I thought it was a foregone conclusion, *you*—but as a matter of fact I didn't just jump to it. Well——'

'Then. . .how?' Len said cautiously.

Philippa licked her lips. 'He told me. . .he. . . Oh, God!' And she swung round on her heel and ran from the room.

Len Colefax stared after her, transfixed, then he started to shake his head in extreme disbelief and to apply to God himself to know *what* he'd done to deserve all this. . .

CHAPTER ELEVEN

PHILIPPA locked herself in her flat for the next two days and was deaf to the phone and the doorbell, although she did let her gently curious landlady know that she was all right but exhausted, and she did ask her to post a letter for her on the first morning.

A letter addressed to Colefax and Carpenter and beginning, 'Dear Sirs', and, 'Without Prejudice'. A letter containing a cheque to cover the costs of her American trip and the terse information that, whatever their decision, she would not be returning. A cheque which left her all but broke and with the bitter knowledge that she would either have to apply to her father for a loan to tide her over until she got another job or sell some of her possessions.

She hardly ate and hardly slept and found she couldn't even think much, and on the third morning discovered it made her tired just to wonder what she would do with the day. But she got up, dressed in a grey tracksuit and was staring out over the garden at the back of the house at grey skies that promised rain when the doorbell rang.

Her first impulse was to ignore it but she was quite sure it would be her landlady, and that that good lady would be thrown into a flutter of concern otherwise.

But it was Mark, in jeans and a royal blue sweater over a check shirt. . . Mark, his grey eyes taking in every detail of her appearance, her pale face, the shadows beneath her eyes, the further weight she'd lost.

'No,' she whispered after what seemed like an age but had only been moments. 'No, no more, please. . .' And she tried to close the door but the floor started to tilt alarmingly beneath her feet, and she wondered dazedly if she was going to faint for the first time in her life.

She didn't, but only due to his presence of mind. He swore beneath his breath and picked her up, carried her over to a chair and lowered her head for a while. Then, as some faint colour came to her cheeks, he let her sit up and began to massage her hands.

He also said roughly, 'What the hell have you been doing to yourself?'

'Nothing. What are you doing here?' She stared at him helplessly. 'There's nothing——' she licked her lips '—we can say to each other now. Not after. . .' She stopped and her shoulders sagged.

'Not after the fiasco of our last couple of meetings, do you mean?' he queried curtly. 'Yes, there is—there has to be. Or doesn't it mean anything to you that I did not in fact marry Susan Bannister?' His eyes were hard and very grey.

'But you let me think——'

'Because it was the first thing that came to mind, wasn't it, Philippa? You never really changed your opinion of me, you still had me lumped in with every faithless, treacherous male you've ever known.'

She took a ragged breath. 'And you,' she whispered, 'let me go through hell first of all, knowing about her——'

'I didn't know you knew,' he said harshly.

'Well, I did.' Her green eyes were bleak and without hope. 'I also knew you were banking on my *not* knowing. Nothing else made sense. And *everything* else seemed to fall into place. Are you trying to tell me you were unaware of what the whole world,' she said bitterly, 'was expecting you to do? You didn't deny it once before.'

'I may not have been unaware of it,' he said with sardonic precision, 'but I was not aware that you would accept Len Colefax's word as gospel on the subject.'

'Ah, but there was so much more, there was Julia, the things you said yourself, the fact that I saw for *myself* the effect you had on Susan,' she said very quietly. 'I saw her looking at you with her heart in her eyes and nothing you can say to me can change that. So, if I misjudged you I'm sorry, but it wasn't without cause when you add it all up. And you've had your revenge—let's leave it at that.'

'And you've never stopped to wonder why I took that revenge, Philippa?' He stared into her eyes.

'I. . .' She shivered, and he noted it with a faint narrowing of his grey eyes. 'Perhaps it was so effective that I didn't. . . I. . .' She stopped and closed her eyes briefly.

'Or,' he said barely audibly, 'stopped to wonder why it was so effective?'

He was still squatting in front of her although he'd laid her hands in her lap minutes before.

'I. . .' But again she couldn't speak and then suddenly she was crying silently and the words came jerkily. 'Yes, but it's no good—don't you understand. . .? I *can't*. . .please, just go away!'

He stood up. 'And I can't do that because I have some explaining to do—I'm going to make you breakfast. Try to relax if you can.'

But she couldn't, and in the end he brought her a glass of neat brandy and made her drink it and eventually it helped, and she lay back in the chair while he began to cook breakfast. But, although she'd stopped trembling and crying, it was as if her mind didn't have the muscle to cope with this turn of events, and she ate bacon and an egg, a slice of toast and honey and drank a cup of hot, strong tea like some sort of automaton. Then she raised her eyes to his over the table and said, 'Thanks. I'll be fine now.'

For a moment his eyes mocked her, then he pulled something from his pocket, let her see it was her cheque, and deliberately tore it up.

That did pierce her numbness briefly. 'I'm still not coming back,' she said flatly.

'No. But, in the meantime, come for a drive with me.'

'A. . .where?'

He shrugged. 'Anywhere.'

She said, stupidly, 'I didn't know you had a car in Brisbane.'

'There's a whole fleet of company cars at my disposal, however.'

She stared at him helplessly. 'Why?'

'I have some things to tell you——'

'Mark——'

But he got up and disappeared into her bedroom and returned with an anorak. 'Come.'

'But. . .' She put a hand to her hair and couldn't even remember if she'd brushed it.

'Your hair looks fine, Philippa,' he said evenly. 'Come.'

He drove down to the coast, an hour's silent drive with her sitting rigidly beside him for the first few miles, then insidiously being soothed by the superb suspension and, incredibly, falling asleep huddled in the corner.

She woke with a jerk and stared about her. At a landscape of sea and grey stormy sky, skyscrapers in the distance, seagulls hovering.

And Mark was watching her, with his arm spread along the back of the seat, his eyes hooded and unreadable, his mouth bracketed with fine lines of tension.

'Oh! Sorry. . .' She sat up. 'Where. . .what. . .?' She pressed her hands together.

'Surfers,' he said. 'I thought, if you feel up to it,

we could walk. It might help to be doing something. It's not raining.'

'All right,' she said dazedly.

And once on the beach, walking beside him but separated by about a foot, she discovered she felt slightly better. As if her battered spirit was responding to the clean, cold air, the crash of the surf, the cries of the gulls, the crunch of the sand underfoot.

He glanced at her after they'd walked in silence for about five minutes, then he said unemotionally, 'Philippa—if I shocked you, I've shocked myself. I've never wanted to hurt anyone quite as much as I wanted to hurt you—or even half or a tenth as much,' he said with bitter irony. 'Because I never cared sufficiently one way or the other for anyone else. Nor, until you left me, did I realise what had happened to me.'

She gradually stopped walking and reluctantly brought her eyes to his face, but they were wary and shadowed still.

He took her hand. 'Keep walking.'

So they started off again, and after a while he said, 'You were more right about me than you guessed, you know—than I guessed. I once said that I did believe love existed, that real, elusive thing, but what I omitted to even tell myself in so many words was that I'd come to believe it wasn't going to exist for *me*, and I didn't realise that when it did it was going to be—so difficult to come to terms with. Why,' he shrugged, 'I let myself lose faith and hope without putting up much of a fight,' he said drily, 'is something we'll have to take into account—it could be a basic character flaw. . .

'So, yes,' he went on, 'I did begin to think that Susan would be as good as anyone else to marry—better than most. At least she was pure and innocent herself. And, yes, I did know it would please my father but not necessarily because of Bannister's—he's not that mercenary and he's genuinely fond of Susan but, well, I suppose it's only human nature to contemplate these things and then——' he grimaced '—it became apparent she was developing an adolescent crush on me—and *everyone* began to hope. My mother, who is lovable but has one burning ambition and that's to see me married and providing heirs for the name; Julia, who was convinced I was going to the dogs and taking one woman after another. . .' He paused. 'And—the idea obviously spread like a ripple. Outside the family, I suspect the main culprit was the inevitable speculation about the future of Bannister's but,' he looked down at her, '*I* never mentioned the subject to a soul.'

Philippa breathed in and out then realised she was counting breaths for some strange reason, as if she wouldn't be able to breathe otherwise.

'Then, taking things unchronologically,' he said in the same even, steady voice, 'my father fell ill and my mother, in her desperation, brought it all out into the open—well, with me. Why was I still holding off? Susan was no longer a child and head over heels in love with me. Didn't I think I owed my father his dearest, maybe dying wish? And Julia had a go too, but the irony there was that she even cited *you* as an example of how I was going to the dogs——'

'Sh—she knew?' Philippa stammered.

'No. Not about us *then*, but she brought up "that girl in the Maldives". We obviously generate some heat, you and I, Philippa.'

She stumbled and he tightened his grasp on her hand. 'But it was then,' he said soberly, 'that I knew that, whatever happened between us, I couldn't marry Susan.'

'Only then?' Philippa whispered.

He laughed briefly. 'Stupid, wasn't it? But in fact it was only then that Susan became a stark reality as opposed to something in the future, something shadowy and, I now realise, unreal. It was also only then that I really understood how everybody had got their hopes up, including my father, including Susan. . .'

'Oh. . .'

'Yes,' he said grimly. 'I don't quite——' He broke off.

'Know how you could have stopped her from falling in love with you? Short of taking to a monastery, neither do I,' Philippa said with a twisted little smile, then she raised her free hand to brush her eyes. 'So. . .?'

'I had to disabuse everyone,' he said drily, 'including Susan, and the only reason I delayed it was because of my father. But in the end he took it well, better than my mother and Julia. Susan. . . Susan said she supposed it might be part of growing up and didn't I think, since she knew it was what her parents would have wanted, that the amalgamation should go ahead? She's had the power to do it since she was eighteen but she's also, in some ways, a more mature nineteen-year-old than I gave her credit for, because when I pointed out to her that some people would think she was too young to make that decision, that she could have been manipulated into it, she said there would no doubt appear to some people to have been a far greater case for manipulation if I'd married her—and anyway, the benefits to Bannister's, which she'd calculated pretty accurately, would answer every critic.'

'Will she be all right?' Philippa asked very quietly.

She heard him sigh. 'I think so. Nineteen is an age for crushes, isn't it?'

They walked in silence until she said huskily, 'And you did all this then discovered I'd run away again?'

'Yes.'

'If—just say your father hadn't become ill when he did, what would have happened to us?'

At last he allowed them to stop walking and he turned her to face him. 'I know now, Philippa,' he said sombrely. 'I'm only sorry I didn't know then.'

'You——' her voice broke '—offered to leave me even while it all must have been going on, rather than make me listen.'

'I suspect that even then I didn't want to believe deep down that I couldn't still walk away from you,' he said with a grim twist to his lips. 'So you were right. I *was* happier for you not to know, but the reason I was clinging to my scepticism was—well, there were several. It was dawning on me that for us it had to be all or nothing, that I'd never be a free man again and yet—you were the one woman who could and had walked away from *me*, Philippa. Even—I know this sounds ridiculous—even the fact that you wouldn't take the Learmonth contract, as such, posed a threat as I saw it.'

Her eyes widened as this sank in, then she was conscious of a desire to bury her face in his royal blue sweater, to be held, but she warned herself that it was too soon and there were things she had to say. . .

'If I was able to walk away from you, it was also because of my own fears. Fears that all my hang-ups would crush what we did have, fears that I'd lose my independence, fears that it wouldn't work for you, the day-in, day-out trivia of marriage. And you deduced that a lot of my cynicism had to do with my family—you were right. My father—well, my mother is nothing more than his glorified housekeeper but she still *loves* him. . . I swore that would never happen to me. Inside of marriage or. . .' She broke off and gestured helplessly with one hand.

'My dear,' he said very quietly, 'let's not delude ourselves—we're *both* strong, independent people, disillusioned to an extent, and there'll be times as there have in the past when we'll probably clash. But,' he stared down at her, 'the simple truth is that I can't live without you now—at least not without being possessed of a rage to repossess you or to hurt you, possessed of a regret for all the years I didn't know you,' he said barely audibly. 'All of which translates to this—I love you, Philippa. Sometimes it may not be comfortable but it's never going to change. It's something,' he brought his hands up to cup her face and smudge her tears, .'that I've never known before. Is it not the same for you?'

It had started to rain, but hesitantly and as if it could well decide to stop, but Philippa was completely unaware of it as she stared into his eyes and saw, perhaps for the first time, his heart. And complete honesty together with his query.

'Yes, it's the same for me,' she whispered. 'What will we do?'

The raindrops were catching in her hair like diamonds and it was curling, and the wind and the chill had brought some colour to her cheeks at last, and her eyes were very green and no longer dazed and uncomprehending but calm at last.

'Do?' he said with an effort. 'Of all the things I'd like to do, there's probably only one we're allowed to do here—but we can go home and do the rest. Such as,' a wry smile lit his eyes, 'sending Len Colefax a telegram to tell him we're getting married, just in case he does have a heart attack.'

Her lips curved into an answering smile. 'I've

been a terrible trial to him—oh, Mark, if the one thing you're allowed to do here is kiss me, would you do it now, please? I. . .'

But he bent his head and claimed her lips and held her as if he'd never let her go.

CHAPTER TWELVE

TWELVE months and two weeks later, on their first wedding anniversary, Philippa and Mark were seated side by side in the back of a vast, chauffeur-driven limousine on their way to a party being thrown for them by Mark's parents.

Philippa was wearing a glittering gown that matched her eyes, and a string of perfectly matched pearls and pearl earrings that had been her anniversary present. Mark was in a dark dinner-suit with a snowy white shirt front, and they were holding hands.

He said. 'Despite your fears about my family resenting you, I think it's safe to say you've won them over completely.'

Philippa smiled faintly and decided not to enlighten him as to the considerable effort on her part it had taken to overcome his arbitrary decision to marry her secretly then present his family with the *fait accompli,* thereby secretly wounding his mother to the core and causing them all to wonder if she was a fortune huntress who had trapped him. She said only, 'I like them. And you can't blame them for wondering about me.'

He grinned wryly then said, 'All things considered, it hasn't been so difficult after all, this marriage.'

Philippa, who had something else on her mind, paused from her inward thoughts and looked backwards mentally and marvelled a little at how it had been, how careful they'd been at first, particularly careful not to crowd each other, treading as if on glass. Until their first row, which had been spectacular and ended up with cold silence for two days then a passionate reunion and, mysteriously, had relaxed them into less care and a closer closeness. Which had slowly grown, and nurtured the knowledge that proximity, strange as it seemed, wasn't going to spoil their love.

'Philippa?'

She looked up to see him examining her with narrowed eyes, and a faint tinge of colour stole into her cheeks. 'Yes. . .?'

'Is something wrong?'

'No. Why?'

'You have,' he paused thoughtfully, 'for the last couple of days had a curiously secretive look in your eyes. And you've been distracted yet—serene. As if you're not altogether with us at the moment.'

'Have I? Well, it might be because our marriage is about to enter a new phase,' she said slowly. 'I wasn't going to tell you yet but——'

'You're pregnant,' he said on a suddenly indrawn breath.

'Well, yes.' She stared into his grey eyes. 'Do you mind?'

'Mind—yes, I do. Charles!' He addressed the

chauffeur peremptorily. 'Turn round and take us back——'

'Mark!'

But back to their Sydney apartment they went in taut silence—it wasn't far, they'd barely travelled two blocks—and, once there, he immediately rang his mother and told her briefly that they'd been delayed.

Then he turned to her, standing in the middle of the lounge in her beautiful green dress, her eyes wide and stunned.

'Mark. . .'

He strolled over to her, a dangerous little glint in his eyes. 'You weren't going to tell me yet?' he said softly. 'Why not? Incidentally, you picked totally the wrong spot to do it, Philippa.'

'You prised it out of me,' she objected. 'But what's so wrong about——?'

'Having it prised out of you in the back seat of a limousine?' he drawled. 'The simple, spectacular effect it has had on me, that's what's wrong. The desire to thoroughly inspect this new territory, to make love to it, to celebrate. . .you're laughing?' He raised an eyebrow at her.

'I'm laughing,' she agreed. 'You had me worried. I thought you might not like the idea.'

'Had you worried,' he repeated. 'Do you really not know yet how much I love you, my beautiful battleaxe?'

'Oh, Mark!' She moved into his arms with a little sigh. But several minutes later she said, 'You don't really mean to. . .?' And looked up into his eyes and that familiar, dangerous little glint in them.

'Yes, I do.' His hands cupped her shoulders then moved to her back and the zip of her dress slipped down.

'But—I'll be a wreck.'

'No, you won't,' he murmured and slid his fingers back up her neck. 'Just late.' He moved his hands again and the green dress slipped off her shoulders. '*I'll* be the wreck if we don't do this. Do you remember intimating to me once that you didn't think this state of affairs could last, Mrs Learmonth?' He stared at the glow of her skin through her black, strapless bra, the shadowed valley between her breasts, then undid the bra and discarded it and raised his eyes to hers.

'Did I intimate that?' she said softly and innocently but she was trembling beneath his touch.

'You certainly did.' He cupped her breasts. 'You even went one step further and theorised on the fact that we couldn't spend all our time in bed——'

'We haven't,' she pointed out but rather dreamily as he teased her nipples, then stared down at them with a faint frown. 'What's wrong?'

'These are changing—do you know, I would have noticed even if you'd decided to be secretive for longer—they wouldn't have escaped my eagle eye, but—what was I saying?'

'You were making me aware that I was wrong about—certain things. I acknowledge it,' she said huskily.

'Good. That's a very admirable quality in a wife. The ability to admit she is in the wrong.'

'You're——' but she was laughing '—impossible sometimes, Mark Learmonth.' And she leant against him, flooded with love. 'So you don't mind?'

'No, Philippa. Do you?' He held her away so he could look deeply into her eyes. 'Motherhood and a career might be hard to juggle.'

Since their marriage, and with his approval, she'd opened her own consultancy firm which had meant she could take as little or as much work as she liked. She said, 'I'll be quite happy to put my career on hold for a time because,' she paused, then told him the truth, 'I think I want this baby more than anything I've ever wanted—except you.'

They were two hours late for their wedding anniversary, but there was something so breathtaking about Philippa, even her mother-in-law couldn't be offended.

In fact, that good lady said thoughtfully to her daughter Julia, 'We might have been wrong about Philippa. What do you think?'

Julia's gaze rested affectionately on her brother and she watched the way he was looking down at his wife. 'Were we ever wrong! They're made for each other, those two,' she said and added, 'Do you think she knew we wondered about her?'

'She won't have to wonder any more,' her mother replied with sudden determination. 'And

I'll tell you something else, Julia. There's a baby on the way.'

Julia looked startled. 'How can you tell?'

Mrs Winston Learmonth looked both wise and complacent. 'I can tell.'

OFFICIAL RULES • MILLION DOLLAR WISHBOOK SWEEPSTAKES
NO PURCHASE OR OBLIGATION NECESSARY TO ENTER

To enter, follow the directions published. If the Wishbook Game Card is missing, hand-print your name and address on a 3" ×5" card and mail to either: Harlequin Wishbook, 3010 Walden Ave., P.O. Box 1867, Buffalo, NY 14269-1867, or Harlequin Wishbook, P.O. Box 609, Fort Erie, Ontario L2A 5X3, and upon receipt of your entry we will assign you Sweepstakes numbers (Limit: one entry per envelope). For eligibility, entries must be received no later than March 31, 1994 and be sent via 1st-class mail. No liability is assumed for printing errors or lost, late or misdirected entries.

To determine winners, the Sweepstakes numbers on submitted entries will be compared against a list of randomly, pre-selected prizewinning numbers. In the event all prizes are not claimed via the return of prizewinning numbers, random drawings will be held from among all other entries received to award unclaimed prizes.

Prizewinners will be determined no later than May 30, 1994. Selection of winning numbers and random drawings are under the supervision of D.L. Blair, Inc., an independent judging organization whose decisions are final. One prize to a family or organization. No substitution will be made for any prize, except as offered. Taxes and duties on all prizes are the sole responsibility of winners. Winners will be notified by mail. Chances of winning are determined by the number of entries distributed and received.

Sweepstakes open to persons 18 years of age or older, except employees and immediate family members of Torstar Corporation, D.L. Blair, Inc., their affiliates, subsidiaries and all other agencies, entities and persons connected with the use, marketing or conduct of this Sweepstakes. All applicable laws and regulations apply. Sweepstakes offer void wherever prohibited by law. Any litigation within the province of Quebec respecting the conduct and awarding of a prize in this Sweepstakes must be submitted to the Régies des Loteries et Courses du Quebec. In order to win a prize, residents of Canada will be required to correctly answer a time-limited arithmetical skill-testing question. Values of all prizes are in U.S. currency.

Winners of major prizes will be obligated to sign and return an affidavit of eligibility and release of liability within 30 days of notification. In the event of non-compliance within this time period, prize may be awarded to an alternate winner. Any prize or prize notification returned as undeliverable will result in the awarding of the prize to an alternate winner. By acceptance of their prize, winners consent to use of their names, photographs or other likenesses for purposes of advertising, trade and promotion on behalf of Torstar Corporation without further compensation, unless prohibited by law.

This Sweepstakes is presented by Torstar Corporation, its subsidiaries and affiliates in conjunction with book, merchandise and/or product offerings. Prizes are as follows: Grand Prize—$1,000,000 (payable at $33,333.33 a year for 30 years). First through Sixth Prizes may be presented in different creative executions, each with the following approximate values: First Prize—$35,000; Second Prize—$10,000; 2 Third Prizes—$5,000 each; 5 Fourth Prizes—$1,000 each; 10 Fifth Prizes—$250 each; 1,000 Sixth Prizes—$100 each. Prizewinners will have the opportunity of selecting any prize offered for that level. A travel-prize option if offered and selected by winner, must be completed within 12 months of selection and is subject to hotel and flight accommodations availability. Torstar Corporation may present this Sweepstakes utilizing names other than Million Dollar Sweepstakes. For a current list of all prize options offered within prize levels and all names the Sweepstakes may utilize, send a self-addressed stamped envelope (WA residents need not affix return postage) to: Million Dollar Sweepstakes Prize Options/Names, P.O. Box 4710, Blair, NE 68009.

For a list of prizewinners (available after July 31, 1994) send a separate, stamped self-addressed envelope to: Million Dollar Sweepstakes Winners, P.O. Box 4728, Blair NE 68009.

The Extra Bonus Prize will be awarded in a random drawing to be conducted no later than 5/30/94 from among all entries received. To qualify, entries must be received by 3/31/94 and comply with published directions. No purchase necessary. For complete rules, send a self-addressed, stamped envelope (WA residents need not affix return postage) to: Extra Bonus Prize Rules, P.O. Box 4600, Blair, NE 68009.

SW9-92